YOU CAN'T SAVE WHAT ISN'T THERE

YOU CAN'T SAVE WHAT ISN'T THERE

A Novella

PAUL MICHAEL ANDERSON

CEMETERY DANCE PUBLICATIONS

Baltimore
2025

"Paul Michael Anderson puts the physical in *metaphysical* portraying the darkly transformative powers of grief and rage in a story where every parent's worst nightmare triggers a monstrous metamorphosis as he places his characters on a looping track of tragedy. Pairing Grand Guignol violence with devastating emotion, *You Can't Save What Isn't There* maximizes readers' pain and shows how facing the truth can often be the most frightening act of all."

—PATRICK BARB, AUTHOR OF *THE CHILDREN'S HORROR*
AND *PRE-APPROVED FOR HAUNTING*

"In *You Can't Save What Isn't There*, Paul Michael Anderson slams us face-first into a gut-wrenching tale of a father's devastation and seemingly justified retaliation. This fast, hard-hitting tale whips us through what happens when we give in to our inner demons and the way grief and anger can change who we once were. It will leave you wondering how you battle back from the worst day of your life and questioning the scars you collect along the way."

—JAMES SABATA, AUTHOR OF *FAT CAMP*

"For some, grief is a process, for others it's a black hole. *You Can't Save What Isn't There* by Paul Michael Anderson is an unapologetic story of one man's descent into darkness. Cal suffers in the wake of his daughter's death, but finds his body beginning to change as he allows his sorrow to overpower the person he'd once been. A fast paced, mysterious, and unflinching read that had me catching my breath in the aftermath of its perfect ending."

—CHRIS PANATIER, AUTHOR OF *THE REDEMPTION OF MORGAN BRIGHT* AND *THE PHLEBOTOMIST*

"Paul Michael Anderson is the modern master of grief horror. *You Can't Save What Isn't There* is a scalpel-sharp and harrowing experience, propulsive in its pacing even as it cuts to your marrow. There's nothing surface level about Anderson's prose, his words a keening cry of loss and rage. Dark, poignant and heartbreakingly brutal—don't miss it."

—LAUREL HIGHTOWER, AUTHOR OF
CROSSROADS AND *THE DAY OF THE DOOR*

"Anderson writes with a sure, steady hand."

—JACK KETCHUM, AUTHOR OF *THE GIRL NEXT DOOR*
AND *THE SECRET LIFE OF SOULS*

"Anderson announces himself as a major talent in the dark fiction realm, capable of fashioning imaginative, bold visions."

—*FANGORIA*

"Paul Michael Anderson's brand of horror is as heart-stopping as it is heart-wrenching."

—GWENDOLYN KISTE, BRAM STOKER AWARD-WINNING AUTHOR
OF *THE RUST MAIDENS* AND *RELUCTANT IMMORTALS*

"Every tale has one thing in common: Anderson's ability to craft a compelling, thought-provoking, dark and beautifully heart-breaking story displaying the darkest depths of the human soul."

—*THIS IS HORROR*

Also By Paul Michael Anderson

Bones Are Made To Be Broken

How We Broke
(co-written with Bracken Macleod)

Standalone

Everything Will Be All Right In The End:
Apocalypse Songs

The Only Way Out Is Through

Cemetery Dance Publications
132B Industry Lane, Unit #7
Forest Hill, MD 21050
www.cemeterydance.com

Trade Paperback Edition

ISBN:
978-1-964780-14-6

Cover Artwork and Design © 2025 by Chris Panatier
Interior Design © 2025 by Desert Isle Design, LLC

For Bracken MacLeod

"Grief is the only eulogy the dead ever hear."
—CHRIS PANATIER, *THE REDEMPTION OF MORGAN BRIGHT*

"Once upon a time" is a phrase synonymous with fairytales—of faraway lands and monarchs and magic and princesses and adventures that delight the eyes, mind, and heart.

This is a fairytale, but the lands are not faraway, the monarch is broken, and the princess is already dead.

Once upon a time.

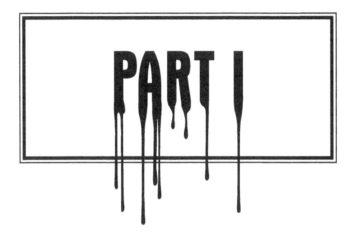

Someone pounded at the apartment door, three solid hits, the kind of knocking that signaled an emergency or the knocker was coming to kick your ass.

Cal leaned out of the bathroom, dressed in boxers. "Who is it?"

Another three solid hits, the door-chain shaking.

Cal glanced at his pocket knife resting on the kitchenette counter. He couldn't think of any emergencies, but he'd burned a lot of bridges over the past two years.

Don't be an asshole, an interior voice said, but his heart was racing all of a sudden, muscles twitchy and nervy with adrenaline.

Something hit the bottom of the door with a soft *thump* as he put his eye to the peephole. He saw his empty apartment hallway, distorted, a line of light brown along the bottom of his view.

"Huh." Frowning, he undid the chain and deadbolts, straining to hear anything on the other side.

Cal gripped the knob. He could picture it—someone standing just to the side, waiting for him. They'd be to the right, so they could swing with their good hand. It was a complete picture, rendered realistically albeit with sharp contrasting colors—the red of the hallway carpet, the green he envisioned the attacker wearing, the paleness of the cocked fist—the way all his ideas used to come when he sat down for the next job.

No one cares, Matheson, the interior voice muttered.

He turned the knob, steeling himself, and yanked the door wide, only for a long rectangular box to fall inward, thumping hard against his hardwood floor. He yipped—it sounded like an ankle-biter dog to his ears—and jumped back, eyes locked on this sudden box half-in and half-out of his door.

It took him longer than it should've to look at the hallway. If there *had* been an attacker, he would've been mincemeat.

"How the fuck did this get here?" he asked, and Robin Roberts on the television laughed behind him.

He stepped around the box and leaned out his door. Nothing, save for the threadbare carpet, more a dull maroon than the vibrant red in Cal's mind, and the electric flambeaux fixtures flickering along the walls. His apartment sat in the middle of the floor, exit stairwells equidistant to either side.

He looked at the box between his bare feet. Someone had left this box, someone big enough to pound a solid wooden door so hard the chain jumped, but had been nimble and quick enough to make themselves scarce.

"Whatever," he breathed. He hunkered and shoved the box the rest of the way into the apartment. A ripple of disgust crossed his face at the feel of the cardboard—furry, the way well-cared-for but old boxes got after a while.

He shut and rebolted the door before turning and facing the box. It was two feet by one foot, maybe six inches deep. A small envelope had been Scotch-taped to the top, where it'd been sealed, baring his full name—*CALVIN MATHESON*—in neat Sharpie, but no return address or shipping information. No labels or logos of any kind.

He hunkered and pulled the envelope free, knuckles brushing the box top. Again that furriness, and he shivered, tearing the envelope open, freeing a single rectangle of cream-colored cardstock. *YOUR CHANCE TO MAKE A CHOICE*, it read, again in Sharpie capitals.

He looked into his cramped living room, straight eyeline to the sole window and its view of the building across the alley. Rain hit the panes in irregular little taps. The television screen threw more light.

"The hell?" Cal muttered, and stood, stepping over the box to where his smartphone sat charging on the kitchenette counter. He swiped his thumb across the screen. No new notifications. He went to texts—one from Jason, confirming today's interview, the next most recent from Maggie's three weeks ago. He didn't bother opening either to read the exchanges. Neither held answers.

He dropped the card and envelope onto the junk mail piling against the counter's edge. Rubbing his fingers together, he bent and grasped the box. Something shifted inside, a whispery rustle, but the box itself was light. He set it on the counter, grabbed his pocket knife to slit through the shipping tape. Pulling the box's sleeves open, a professionally folded black suit rested in a clear dry-cleaning bag, complete with a white shirt and blood-red tie. Along the bottom, also in clear plastic, were two black wingtip shoes, polished brightly. A belt and pair of black socks sat within the shoes.

Cal's eyes ticked over this, chewing on the inside of his cheek. He didn't know enough about suits—off-the-rack was the closest he'd ever gotten—but he tore a hole into the bag and thumbed open the shirt collar, then the jacket. No labels.

Brow furrowing, Cal unsheathed the shoes from their plastic bags. The shoes lacked a label under the tongue, and the belt under the buckle. Frowning, he removed the pants and unfolded them, but there was just a size label—34X30, in gold stitching—along the inner waistband. The coat had a similar size label—17 1/2—against the inside pocket.

"What the fuck, friends and neighbors," he muttered, dropping the pants back into the box. He picked his phone back up, went to his email this time. Maybe he'd ordered something while drunk. That'd happened more than once over the past few months; he'd woken up one afternoon to find three boxes from Amazon stacked beside his door. Only encroaching poverty had sobered him up.

Where would you have ordered a fucking suit like this, to be delivered in this cryptic-ass way? the interior voice growled.

There wasn't anything in his inbox, nor his sent messages, trash, or even his spam folder. On the television behind him, *Good Morning America* went to the local affiliate for the half-hour newsbreak.

YOU CAN'T SAVE WHAT ISN'T THERE

He debated going back to his texts, of asking Jason or Maggie if they had done this. They were the only two people still talking to him, but while Jason could still be considered a friend, Maggie most assuredly could not. He set the phone down.

"Whose fault is this?" He shook his head. He had to be on the street by no later than eight if he wanted to get uptown in time.

He went to his bedroom, where he kept the blinds closed and the shadows grew like mold along the corners and seams. He flicked the light and faced his open closet. This was a formal interview, with strangers, and a button-down flannel and khakis weren't going to work. His one suit, Navy blue, hung lopsided to one side, but he hadn't worn that since—

He shook his head again, listlessly picked up his sandy brown Dockers shoes. Even if they were professional enough—and they were five years too-old and too-scuffed for that—it wouldn't do for this meeting.

"Dress for the job you want," he muttered. He dropped the shoes and leaned his forehead against the closet door-frame. He'd junked ninety-five percent of his belongings when he'd moved from his post-divorce condo to this shitty apartment. He hadn't been thinking straight, of course. They always said kids couldn't conceive of forever, or long term, and Cal was here to tell the world that the same thing was true with adults, especially adults who were dealing with—

Cal slammed his fist into the frame, pain derailing the train of thought. He pushed himself off the wall and went back into the main room where the black suit sat like an inevitability while Robin Roberts told viewers what to expect in the eight o'clock hour.

He gritted his teeth. Like someone had known, he thought. Like...

Get the fuck on with it, the interior voice ordered.

"Whatever," he breathed, and quickly got dressed, his hardened expression dissolving into confusion as he realized how *well* everything fit, like it had been molded solely for his body type. He'd *never* worn clothes like this. He wasn't the most put-together of people, even at the best of times, but he'd never been slovenly. Still, knotting his tie—and it only took one try to get that double-Windsor down, a rare feat— and throwing on the jacket, he appeared like a revelation in the water-specked hall mirror.

"Can almost hear Elise clapping," he said, the words just appearing in his mouth, and that brought him up so short so suddenly, it was like an invisible dog chain had been yanked by a cruel owner. His face grew red hot, his vision blurring and throat clogging.

Cal stumbled. "No, no, *no*..." He shoved the empty box into the kitchenette, where it clattered against the dirty pots on the stovetop, and rested his elbows on the counter, using the heels of his hands to grind into his eyes.

He took a deep breath, then another, then another. "I'm okay," he grunted. "I'm okay."

He sighed, rolled his shoulders, and then shot the cuffs of his shirt. Something tiny but sharp poked at his inner wrist, and he hissed. He brought his wrist up, but couldn't see anything. "Huh."

YOU CAN'T SAVE WHAT ISN'T THERE

He shoved his phone and his keys into his pockets. He eyed his pocket knife—intentionally not focusing on the TO DAD inscription on the handle. He *didn't* live in the best of neighborhoods. Still, the idea of him wielding off nefarious attackers with what amounted to a letter-opener with delusions of grandeur was absurd enough that he grinned. *Ah, yes, Cal Matheson,* he could hear Maggie deadpanning. *Hathaway's answer to a warrior of righteous justice.*

A memory of Elise laughing, that little girl laugh that still held ghost-notes of toddlerhood, and the smile soured while it was still blooming on his face. He left the television on, grabbing the portfolio satchel leaning against the wall next to it.

"Wish me luck," he said, and the intro music of *Good Morning America* seemed to applaud him.

Cal watched the business-casually dressed man on the other side of the massive desk, in an office that could've housed Cal's entire apartment, flipping through Cal's portfolio and realized he couldn't remember the man's name. The name of the company—GuruYou, something hip and reflexively stupid—floated into the front of his mind, and Cal clung to it like a shipwreck survivor clinging to floating wreckage. He felt a muscle jump in his cheek.

The man closed Cal's portfolio and tossed it onto his blotter. "I don't usually take head-hunting tips from legal, but after Jason forwarded me some old thumbnails, I had to meet you." He leaned back in his leather chair, throwing a knee against the edge of his desk. He wore khakis. "College roommates, he said?"

"When we were undergrads," Cal replied. "I was graphic design, Jason was pre-law."

The man nodded towards Cal's suit. "You look like one of our lawyers."

Cal kept his hands on the arms of the chair. "I wanted to make a good impression."

The man sat up and tapped Cal's portfolio. "This does it, honestly. We do a lot of media here, a lot of digital, but there's still a large segment that goes print—or can transition between print and digital. You're like what would happen if Norman Rockwell had been introduced to Photoshop."

Probably the one artist he knows, the interior voice growled, but Cal said, "It's like any industry, you have to keep up." He nodded towards the portfolio. "Some of those started as sketches that I either scanned into or redid entirely in Clip Studio Paint Ex, which a lot of professional comic artists use."

Cal watched the man's eyes glaze. Ad whores. They were all the same.

The man pulled a sheet from the portfolio's side closer. "I was reviewing your CV, you worked for some good agencies, but there's a sizable gap between last firm and now...? I asked Jason, but he wasn't very forthcoming."

Cal cleared his throat. He'd thought this might come up, had prepared an answer for it, but actually having to use it made his chest feel dry and dusty, like an attic that hadn't been explored in a while and left to bake in the summer heat "My daughter died a little over a year ago in an accident. Her mother and I are divorced and I...wasn't there." He couldn't help glancing at his hands, gripping the arms of the seat.

"I—" the man started to say, the muscles twitching around his eyes. You don't look for a lie in the eyes, Cal thought, but what happens around them. Same with honest reactions. "I'm sorry to hear that, Calvin. Truly I am." He looked away, at the bank of windows to the side that offered a view of downtown.

Cal swallowed. He storyboarded leaning forward and rabbit-punching the man in the face—once, twice, three times, until he felt bone and cartilage crack and saw blood spurt—and shifted slightly in his seat. Something pricked his side—he hadn't checked if all the tailoring pins had been removed. He frowned. Must be it.

"No one prepares you for it," he said in an even voice that felt more startling to him than the prick in his side, "but I'm still here, and I've always loved my work."

The man cleared his throat. "Well, I think we can help on that end. I'm going to call Janet, our head of HR, after we're done here, prepare our offer package." He tried on a smile that looked pulled by fish hooks, and he slid Cal's portfolio across the desk. "You should hear from her this afternoon, at the latest, and if all looks good, we'll try to get you back into the saddle next week."

Cal stood, taking hold of his portfolio. "Thank you."

The man stood with him. "No, thank *you*—I think we're going to do great things together." He put his hand out. Cal shifted his portfolio to the hand grasping his satchel, and gave him a brisk double-pump. The man's hands were moisturized, free of jewelry, compared to Cal's rough, chapped ones.

"Welcome to GuruYou," the man said somehow with a straight face.

"I look forward to getting to work," Cal said. "Thank you." He started for the door, which opened and a woman roughly the man's age entered.

"Hi, Greg, sorry to interrupt—"

"You're good," the man—Greg—said from behind Cal. "We were finishing up."

Cal slid around the woman. Greg. The name fit, the artificial prick. A nothing name for a nothing person, the kind that would absorb the work of others, not understanding anything but the product itself, just so they could then claim the credit. Something pricked him again, his shoulder this time, as he stepped into the hallway. He had to go over the suit when he got home. He felt like a voodoo doll.

Cal mule-kicked the apartment door closed as he sent off a thank-you text to Jason. Standing in the entryway, he hesitated, then swiped to his last conversation with Maggie. Keeping his eyes locked on the keyboard, he typed, *Got a new gig with a firm. Dumb name. Good pay.*

His thumb paused over the paper-airplane symbol. He ground his teeth, then typed, *Hope you and Dennis are doing okay.*

YOU CAN'T SAVE WHAT ISN'T THERE

He hit SEND, then tossed his phone onto the kitchenette counter.

"Shit," he said. Deep breath, then, "I'm okay. I'm doing okay." He shook his head and dropped his satchel against the wall between the television and archway to the bedroom and bath.

Thoughts built like storm clouds in the back of his mind, the same looming tension he always felt when left to his own devices, but he focused on the next steps, then the steps after that—get this suit back into its dry cleaner bag before he ruined it, hang it in the closet.

He pulled the knot away from his throat, and his stomach twisted, like someone's massive fist had reached in and squeezed. He grunted, clammy sweat bursting along his hairline. His hands left the tie, grasping the archway to stay upright, and his stomach settled.

Cal paused there, slightly hunched. "The hell?" He couldn't remember the last time he'd eaten anything, just coffee, but that wasn't a hunger pang by any stretch of the imagination. When he looked at his hands, they trembled slightly.

He shook them briskly. "Get it together," he said, then pulled the tie's knot free with quick, jerky movements.

The pain came in a thunderclap, the hand returning to crush his organs and drive the pulp up his throat. Cal gagged and shambled into the bathroom, going to his knees in front of his toilet. He vomited, eyes squeezed closed, his guts turning and twisting.

Finally, when he was reduced to just panting, he opened his eyes to see blood sloshing in the bowl.

"Jesus," he croaked, recoiling and slamming his back against the side of his tub. The thought was immediate—*Cancer, it's cancer, has to be, eating me alive*—and the equally immediate attempt to correct it fell flat. His schedule of annual physicals had always been slipshod, and he couldn't remember going to one since before his divorce. But, still, did cancer really work that fast, with no sign whatsoever until you crashed, to continue the metaphor, into a billboard like stabbing pain and a toilet full of bloody bile?

The tone of his thoughts, that hectoring sarcasm that Maggie found charming over a decade ago but had worn thin years after, calmed him more than the actual content of his thinking. He wiped his nose with his jacket sleeve like a kid. The strange, perfectly tailored suit swaddled him, suffocating, and he thrashed over the old linoleum, struggling to get out of his jacket.

He freed his shoulders when the stabbing began—instead of quick jabs like before in scattered places, what felt like millions of little serrated knives *diving* into his torso. He looked down to see the perfectly white shirt break out into a garden of blood blossoms and screamed as much from the sight as from the pain. Black bordered his vision, which kaleidoscoped as he went limp, passing out before his head thunked the bathroom floor.

His phone *ding*-ed with a new notification, pulling Cal back from unconsciousness to find himself on the bathroom floor, his head out the doorway and staring up at the water-marked ceiling. He heard the measured tones of a newscaster on television. The heavy tang of sweat and wet meat hung thick in the air.

His thoughts tumbled, not quite connecting. His skull felt like it'd replaced his brain with wet cement and raising his head was a chore. Every inch of his upper body felt sore and ill-used. Tenderized. His shirt was soaked with drying blood, but all he could do was blink at this for a moment.

"What...the fuck..." he croaked, his voice cracked and thick, and began working to push himself into a sitting position. His body sent warnings along his nerve-endings, cautioning him to stay still, but he threw a numb hand out, grasping the sink to keep himself upright. Something made a *clink* sound, and he blinked at the pen he held, pressed awkwardly between his hand and the porcelain edge. When had he pulled a pen from his pocket? Why? Before he could consider those questions, his stomach rolled over languidly, filling his mouth with thick, viscous spit.

Behind him, his phone *ding*-ed again. Then again. And again.

Cal pulled himself to his knees, dropping the pen and clinging to the edge of the sink like a penitent before a holy altar. If he'd been able to step out of the moment and observe himself, he might've noted that, for once, he wasn't thinking of Elise or Maggie and Dennis, wasn't thinking through the kind of simmering, despairing rage that had become his base-line for so long.

He looked into the toilet. The bloody, chunky water had calmed, and its stench had combined with the vinegar reek of old urine. His stomach rolled over again, and he batted the toilet lid closed. His jacket had landed between the toilet and his tub, and he clung to the sink while reaching for it. Vertigo filled the base of his skull as his fingertips brushed fabric. He forced a deep breath and stretched further, grabbing the jacket. When he pulled the jacket to him, the vertigo disappeared, and when he opened his eyes, he could see clearer.

"Fuck," he breathed. "What the fuck."

He pulled himself upright. His visage in the mirror was a horrorshow of pale skin and sweaty messy hair and darkened eye sockets. Like a Tim Burton character. Errant blood dotted the sides of his mouth, the underside of his jaw. Two small rash-like marks stood at the edge of his hairline, to either side of his widow's peak.

"Fucking hell," he said. Questions circulated like autumn leaves in a high wind, but nothing he could grasp fully and nothing he could answer, anyway. He dropped the jacket onto the toilet lid. His stomach flipped again, the vertigo twigging his vision, and he swayed on his feet.

"Get it the fuck *together*," he snarled at his reflection. His teeth were pink, and anger bubbled through him. He hugged it close. If there was one thing he'd learned, anger was a motivator. Anger kept you grounded. Anger didn't give a damn about the hows and whys—it only cared about eliminating whatever it was that had brought the anger forth.

Cal washed his hands under steaming water. For just an instant, his skin became black and leathery, his nails transformed into dark claws.

YOU CAN'T SAVE WHAT ISN'T THERE

"Fuck!" he cried, recoiling. The vertigo pounced, and his back slammed into the bathroom doorway. He grasped the door itself to keep his balance, and when he looked down, his hands were normal, if a little pink from the heat. He put one against his quaking stomach, rewetting the bloodstains.

Taking deep breaths, he shut off the water and grabbed his jacket. The feel of the fabric beneath his fingertips sent a calm wave through his gut. "Shit," he breathed, staring at the floor between his bathroom and kitchenette the way a man abandoned in the desert without resources might consider the horizon. The tie lay like a desiccated snake in the archway.

Swallowing hard, he took a step and didn't fall over. He took another. His legs felt rickety, Popsicle sticks held with Elmer's glue—

—like Elise's crafts, his interior voice murmured—

—stop that, *stop that*, the rest of his brain replied—

—but he kept upright, going to the archway and, using it for support, bending down and grabbing his tie with the hand holding his balled-up jacket. When he straightened, he felt more solid, more grounded, the way one feels when they're not yet a hundred-percent after an illness, but they were making progress. His phone *beeped*, accusatory.

"Fuck," he hissed, but he was able to walk over to his kitchenette and grab his phone. He tapped the screen as it *dinged* again, and he had four notifications—messages from Jason and Maggie, a missed call, and a new voicemail.

"Lookit mister popularity over here," he grunted, and swiped away the lock screen. He went to calls first—the missed call wasn't in his contacts, but had the 814 area code of the city—then his voicemail.

"Good afternoon, Mr. Matheson," a woman said. "I'm Janet Harding from GuruYou personnel? I wanted to call and alert you that our offer package has been emailed to the address on your resume through DocuSign. If you could review the materials and, if they're satisfactory, sign your agreement, we can get you into the office as early as Monday, but if you have any questions, don't hesitate to call me at—"

She rattled off her number, but Cal hit 7 to delete, then closed out the call.

He shifted the wad of clothes under his arm, and his interior voice asked, *Why not set those down?* But his mind skittered away from that.

He went to his text, glancing at Maggie's bolded name before hitting Jason—*just heard from Greg congrats dude! cant wait to work with you! you owe me a drink!*

Cal grunted, swiped back to his message home page. His eyes lingered over Maggie's name, and the (3) that stood next to it. He could see a bit of the message—*Congratulations! I'm so...*—and he almost just deleted it. He couldn't for the life of him think of why she would send multiple messages, or that any of them would be any good. Their one child together was dead, they'd been divorced for years, so why were they bothering playing nice with each other, or even bothering talking at all?

Cal shut his eyes. "You texted her first, you asshole," he said. "Don't be such a fucking coward."

YOU CAN'T SAVE WHAT ISN'T THERE

He hissed air through his teeth, and opened Maggie's message. The first read, *Congratulations! I'm so happy for you, Calvin!*, and that was okay, but the second was a picture of Elise's gravestone, a pinkish gray marble rectangle with rough sides and top. Cal blinked and his eyes were burning, wet, as he took in the chiseled angel and flowers, the inscription beneath:

Elise Anna Matheson
Loved Daughter
April 11, 2014 – May 20, 2021.

He saw the fresh blossoms and tilled earth in front, but his gaze locked onto the two shadows thrown across the stone. One was his wife. The other would be her husband, Dennis.

The smartphone's case squeaked beneath his grip, and his eyes dropped to the third message. *Went to visit Elise yesterday,* Maggie wrote. *We would've invited you, but didn't think you'd want to go, or were ready.*

"We," Cal said through his teeth. His phone case squeaked some more. "*We. We* didn't think you'd want to go. *We* would've invited you."

The tears were scalding, hotter than the water he'd washed his hands with. His vision deteriorated until the room was a mess of hued blobs. His lips peeled back from his grinding teeth as he hissed air in and out like an overwhelmed engine. Heat climbed his throat, built into the back of his mouth.

He threw the phone into the living room, where it slammed into the wall beside the window. *"THERE IS NO WE, YOU FUCKING CUNT!"* he shrieked. *"YOU*

MOTHERFUCKERING MURDERERS!" He roared, an inarticulate bellow of pain and rage.

When Cal ran out of air, grief came in like a sucker punch, clawing at his brain and chest. He staggered, ass hitting the stove, and his knees unhinged. He slid down, already sobbing, hugging the balled jacket and tie like a child with a cuddle, burying his face into the fabric. The noises coming out were painful to hear.

Cal was still crying when, for the second time that day, he passed out.

It's a dream, he knows it's a dream, and that knowledge fills him with sadness because it's the first good dream he's had in...he doesn't know how long.

He sits at his old design table, the duck-neck lamp in the corner clicked on and casting a warm yellow cone over what he'd been drawing, but he's not looking at that—he's looking at Elise, wearing the same dress she'd worn in her last school photos, the one she called her blue picnic blanket dress with the wide straps. She stands in front of the window, full of mellow spring morning sunshine, and he realizes that he's in his apartment; somehow he's gotten his design table back, his daughter back, but he's still in this shitty apartment. Warmth fills him, anyway, starting in his chest, traveling down into his gut and up into his head. It doesn't matter, does it, where this dream takes place?

No, it doesn't matter, Daddy, Elise says, shaking her head slightly, the curly mess of her hair—Maggie's contribution to

YOU CAN'T SAVE WHAT ISN'T THERE

their daughter's genetic makeup—bouncing. You're drawing again! Isn't that great? *But then her mouth does something strange—his mind thinks of glitches in film—and she adds,* You look really handsome, Daddy.

He frowns because the words *sound familiar, the way she said them, but not here. She never said them* here, *and he—*

It doesn't *matter,* Daddy, *she repeats, little girl firmness showing through.* Look at how *good* you're doing! You just have to keep doing your very best, and you are! Keep making good choices!

That's something he and Maggie used to say to her, and he'd always found it funny how children parrot their folks, but his heart starts beating too fast, no longer sad or warm, but scared instead. He looks like Elise asked, looks at what he's drawn, and the scream builds in his chest, distends his throat with its size, because he's drawn a monster, a black horror of thick claws to rend and massive spiraled horns to pierce the sky, and it's wearing a suit like his, and Cal screams, he screams, not in pain or anger or loss, but sheer terror—

Cal jerked awake, back thumping the front of the couch, knees knocking the underside of the coffee table. His hand clenched, snapping the pencil in half. He stared at the pieces quizzically as they fell onto the sheaf of copy-paper in front of him. When he saw what had been drawn there, he jerked again, more violently, the suit jacket pulling tight around his shoulders, tie digging into his neck—

(??jacket??)

(???tie???)

He looked down at himself and saw he was fully dressed in the suit again, but the suit was immaculate, the white shirt as pure as Ivory soap, the tie double-Windsor'ed again.

"What the *fuck?*" he cried, looking around. He'd been crying in the kitchen, hadn't he? Achy and covered in blood and sick to his stomach. And then he must've fallen asleep, right, and—

(dreamed of Elise)

(it doesn't matter Daddy)

(you're drawing again)

(making good choices)

—woke up wedged between the coffee table and couch, the way he'd sat as a kid, drawing.

Drawing...

Cal shuffled through the half-dozen or so pages of printer paper with shaking hands. Aside from one, the bottom, each page was spread out like a comic book sequence—roughly etched-out panels of alternating sizes descending the sheet, over and over, drawn in heavy lines. Cal's eyes flicked to the snapped pencil, saw the tip was rounded and needed sharpening. Beyond the sheets, three more pencils waited, also worn down.

Cal leaned back, his gaze unable to hold onto any one item for very long. He'd dreamed of Elise, he'd dreamed of making art again, and it hadn't been a very long dream, he thought, but apparently long enough to not only draw for an extended length of time, but to do so with the foresight to have multiple pencils ready, because to sharpen during the experience would've...what? Woken him up?

Something—not in his gut, but in his chest—said this was right.

"Why, though?" he breathed, and someone on television, which was still on, gasped. He looked up—afternoon soap operas.

He swallowed hard, trying to control the heavy, fast pacing of his heart, and leaned forward. Up until Elise's death, he'd always drawn, even as his career had had him rely more and more on the digital end of the creative toolbox. Sometimes it was a doodle on a menu, or something sketched while in a pitch meeting. Often, while Elise would watch morning cartoons, he'd sit beside her on the couch with a reporter's notepad and start with shapes that would grow and shift and become bizarre Byzantine designs and creatures. He remembered the Elise's frequent delight when she'd notice what she called his "morning pictures."

He smiled himself, now, as heat filled his cheeks and the edges of his eyes turned gritty and wet. He'd stopped drawing after her death.

The style used on the pages reminded him of things he'd done as an undergraduate, when he'd gotten through art history and theory only by consuming equal amounts of underground comics and what he'd called "cape" books. The angles of Norm Breyfogle and heavy shadowed lines of Bernie Wrightson.

Every wordless panel on these new pages took the perspective of what he'd always called the "heaven angle", looking down at the focus of the picture. On the top page, he'd drawn an elementary school turnaround, where kids, quick humanoid flicks with his pencils, milled on the sidewalks and lawns and the curved lane was chock-a-block with boxy cars and school buses.

The panels descended, the "camera" zooming in, to one particular pair—Elise, holding the hand of her teacher at the edge of the curb...what had been her name?

Cal looked up, squinting. Her husband had taken a swing at him at the school memorial service...Flaherty. That'd been it. Mrs. Flaherty. First grade teacher. Elise had called her Mrs. Flowery.

That pained smile touched the corners of Cal's mouth again, and he looked back down at the papers. The panels zoomed in steadily until they were in the extreme foreground with the other kids and objects rendered soft and ill-focused in the extreme back—a medium shot to show Flaherty looking down at Elise looking up. The last panel a medium shot of just Elise, wearing the dress in his dream, her dark curly hair a nest on top of her head. Below the panel, not so much as drawn as gouged into the paper, a sound effect: *SCCRRRREEEEEEEEEEEEECHHH*. What had made that sound? He'd woken up before he could go to the next page.

Tears filled Cal's eyes. He pulled his knees up to his chest. "Oh god. Oh my god..."

He batted away the top page, then the papers beneath, until he got to the bottom sheet, the only one not drawn as a comics spread. A mockup cover—Elise, standing with her back to the "camera", facing and looking up at what looked like a chaotic maelstrom, fragmented like a stained-glass window. He'd sketched in some of the "panes" to indicate which ones should be darker or lighter. Along the top, he'd roughly designed *ELISE MATHESON AND HER INCREDIBLE INTERDIMENSIONAL JOURNEY* in dramatic lettering.

Cal closed his eyes and curled into himself, sobs coming in hot and wet, but not in the uncontrolled state that'd led him to pass out before. A throbbing ache crackled through his heart and mind, flexing and pulling at the nerve-endings in between. His head filled with pressure, only nominally lessened with each shuddering gasp for air. A humming moan underscored it all, banishing any thought and leaving just the dark expanse of an aching mind.

Finally, his body relaxed a bit from being one single clenched muscle, and he opened his eyes, taking the scene in front of him in total. At one point, long after Elise's death but long before now, he'd begun to feel like he'd turned a corner on his grief and rage, where, for a few days, maybe a week, he hadn't felt like his brain had been replaced by a wasp's nest that had been briskly shaken. During that brief, calm period, he'd imagined returning to art—not graphic design, but a graphic novel. Comics had been what had gotten him into art in the first place, and it'd always been his emotional refuge. Why not channel his lingering emotions into a full story? He had enough contacts to pitch it, either to an indie press or an agent. He'd tell a story of his daughter. It'd be a sad story, of course, emotional, but he, an atheist through and through, could imagine what had happened to his daughter after her death, give her life, even if it was only in the confines of his imagination and the printed page. He'd channel that hurt into something beautiful, for her, so she could live on.

But the brief respite in pain had ended with a thunderclap—not any one particular event occurring, but just the end of the calm—and as he'd sunk back into it, existing only on what he'd saved and kept financially from the divorce, he'd forgotten all about it.

His eyes went to the title again: *Elise Matheson And Her Incredible Interdimensional Journey.* God, why had that returned all of a sudden?

"Why any of it?" he muttered, muffled by his hands. He could feel the suit, the damned suit, whispering against him. No pinpricks now, but what would happen if he tried to take the suit off again? His skin, whole and without pain, rippled with gooseflesh at the idea.

He dropped his hands, took a shaky breath. "That couldn't have happened," he said, and his voice was firm and brooked no argument, but it also carried no weight. Forget that somehow he'd been re-dressed as he slept (and drew, apparently)—he'd *felt* the pain and vertigo and nausea, had *seen* the blood soak through his shirt. Even at his most drunken, he'd *never* hallucinated before, and he was stone sober now, had been since realizing he either had to kill himself or get a job again.

"Then what the fuck is going on here?" he asked, but neither the television or his interior voice gave him an answer.

His smartphone rang off to the left, making him jump and knock the coffee table. The pencils rolled and fell to the floor with a clatter.

YOU CAN'T SAVE WHAT ISN'T THERE

"Jesus, Matheson," he muttered, and got himself out from the wedge of space. The backs of his legs pricked with pins-and-needles and he hobbled over to the window, where his phone vibrated in an oblong of gray-white light, a corner of his protective cover dusted in drywall. He squinted at the hairline crack of the screen, and saw JASON on the caller ID.

Grunting, he scooped up the phone and pushed ACCEPT. "Hello?"

"Hey, motherfucker!" Jason cried into his ear. "Congratulations, man! I'm so fucking happy for you. I knew Greg would love your shit—who wouldn't, brother? Shit yeah, work buddies!"

Cal's mouth twitched. Jason was part of legal counsel for a metropolitan ad firm, pulled in six figures easily, but when he talked to Cal, he still sounded 19 and perpetually on the hunt for the next drink and lay.

"Yeah, man," Cal said. "Thanks. Thank you. It means a lot. Really."

"Don't fucking sweat it, Cal. *You* got yourself the job with your skill, bro. I just opened the door." Here, his voice lost some of his sports-stadium rah-rah-rah volume. "I'm just glad to help, ya know? You were in a bad place—for good reason; I would've lost my fucking mind, man—but you *are* my brother, and I needed to help."

Cal wiped his forehead, and, to his credit, his hand didn't shake all that much. "I know, and it's appreciated."

"You good? I mean, right now. You feel good?"

"I feel..." He glanced at the sheaf of papers on his coffee table, then shook his head. "I feel...okay. Shaky. But, okay."

"*Good,*" Jason replied, and he sounded like an adult, finally. "Does that mean you feel social?"

"What does *that* mean?"

"I mean, do you wanna come out tonight?" Jason asked, then added quickly, "I don't mean clubbing, or anything—shit, we're too old for that—but a bunch of us from the firm get together on Friday nights to have a drink and relax a little. Good folks, not just lawyers, and I could introduce to some of the people you're gonna be working with." Another brief pause, "I mean, you *are* accepting the offer, right? I guess I should've asked instead of assuming, but—"

Cal closed his eyes. "I'm accepting it. Of course I am. Between the divorce and...and everything else, I don't have much choice, do I?"

"Love the enthusiasm, Cal."

"You know what I fucking mean, dipshit." He added a chuckle so it didn't come off as too mean.

Jason responded with an actual laugh. "Good, man. Good. But, anyway, did you wanna come meet and greet? No pressure, and I don't know if you already got plans, but—"

Cal's gaze lingered on the drawings. He'd junked his old design table when he'd moved in here because, just like children, grieving parents can't conceive of forever. "No, I don't have plans." He took a breath. "Sure. Sure, I'll come out."

"Fucking *awesome*, fam!" The speaker crackled. "We meet at this place called Walter's, just a few blocks down from GuruYou—"

"That's a stupid name, by the way."

YOU CAN'T SAVE WHAT ISN'T THERE

"Yeah, but the check's clear. Anyway, it's on Wood Street, near Fifth. Think you can find it?"

"I know the area."

"Of course you do. It's almost four, now. See you there at...six?"

He swallowed. "Sounds great. I owe you the first drink."

"Damned skippy you do. See you at six, man."

Cal disconnected and let his arm drop. He took in his living room, the television beginning the final commercial run before the four o'clock news, the scattering of art on his out-of-place coffee table, and, finally, down at his black suit, impeccable still.

"What the fuck is going on?" he asked the apartment, but nothing inside or out, had any answers for him.

Cal let the post-work bar conversation flow past him— pieces of office gossip, blue skying upcoming projects and campaigns, spouses and kids, plans for the weekend. Jason sat across from him at the cocktail table, tie and suit jacket gone, leaning to talk to a woman roughly their age at the table to his left, who sat with two men, also suited. A table to Cal's right also had three people.

Cal shifted in his chair, back against the wall, watching. The main room was a narrow rectangle, long end extending from the street, done in honey-colored wood with electric *flambeaux* that reminded Cal of the ones in his apartment building, but on steroids. The bar itself was a small rectangle, every stool taken while three college-aged bartenders in puffy white shirts and black armbands worked the circuit beneath two tilted flatscreen televisions, both silent. Most of the booths and other tables were filled, all around Cal's age or younger. A professional place, a waystation between the drudge of the workday and whatever awaited them at home.

A comfortably warm buzz filled his midsection. This felt *good*, though to articulate that, even just to himself, seemed strange and off-putting to him. Here, the weirdness of the day seemed more dream than reality, in spite of still wearing the suit with jacket still on and tie still knotted.

One of Jason's coworkers—one of his, too, he supposed, although he couldn't tell in what function—leaned in. "So, Jason told me you were responsible for that children's hospital campaign a few years back."

Cal nodded. "I was lead designer, but I was part of a team."

"It looked good. Flashy. Those ads on the bus stops really contrasted with everything around it. The photos—"

Cal took a sip of his bottle of beer. "That was a colleague of mine—Lisa Hoelsher. Her and a few others handled the, y'know, the *big* ads—billboards and bus stops and marques. We'd learned that people reacted more favorably, actually *saw* the ads, if they were photo-realistic instead of artistic. Art in big splashes tends to kinda blur in the eye. My half of the team handled mailers and the dailies and magazine ads, and those were more artsy because—"

"In smaller areas, *art* tends to contrast," the guy finished, nodding. "That's really smart stuff, Calvin. Or do you prefer Cal?"

YOU CAN'T SAVE WHAT ISN'T THERE

"Whichever."

This *did* feel good, and the longer it went on, the easier it got to admit to himself. Forget the weirdness of *today*, *everything* since Elise died felt suddenly hazy and ill-focused, with only awful milestones rising from the fog, like things remembered in the height of a dizzying fever. He'd come out the other side, maybe—not the false eye-of-the-storm calm he'd felt when he'd initially dreamed up a graphic novel as a way of handling his grief—but a real chance of getting out from under the storm clouds that had hovered over him for so long.

He relaxed a little in his seat, listening to Jason explain a has-to-be-bullshit story of going to Niagara Falls a few years back, hand going to the tie knot. He loosened the knot from his Adam's Apple, and the fuzzy warm feeling in his gut changed to an acidic churn the way a flame changed color when you added phosphorus.

Cal stiffened in his chair. His hand dropped away from his tie, going to his pocket, where it pulled a pen. It did this automatically, as his mind wrapped itself around the shift in his midsection, and some dim part of him feeling grateful that, even when he'd stopped drawing, he'd never stopped carrying a pen. He leaned forward, earning another sloshing turn in his gut. He gritted his teeth as his other hand, also acting automatically, pulled a cocktail napkin from the stack. He started drawing, light blue lines hesitant against the fragile material. The sounds of the bar around him faded to a droning hum in the back of his mind, his focus locking in on the napkin the way carriage horses wore blinders to see only what was in front of him.

He worked quickly, not thinking about what his hand was doing, just letting it work. As the picture took shape—he was drawing the bar itself, the suits crowded around it rendered as dark silhouettes, with the focus on the bartenders, lit from above, leaning into his Wrightson influence—the churn lessened, faded to nothing. As it did, and the picture solidified beneath his pen, the blinders left his eyes and the bar sounds rose in volume and distinction.

"Holy shit, dude," Jason said, and Cal looked up to see his old college roommate staring.

"What?" His voice sounded like too much of a croak to his ears.

"*That*, dude." Jason pointed. "You did that like it was *nothing* in, like, five minutes."

Cal looked down at the sketch. The perspective wasn't quite right, a little too abrupt, and some of the shadowing appeared to go in contradictory directions, but his free hand went to his gut beneath the table. Not a single burble. He swallowed hard. Drawing had been an automatic move for him, like...his mind struggled with an apt comparison. Like taking aspirin when you felt a headache slam into you.

"I've always doodled," he said. "You know that."

"Fuck, must've forgotten." He shook his head and tapped the woman he'd been talking to. "Jules, look at this. *Shit*."

Jules did, and her eyes widened slightly. "Okay, you're on *my* team for every campaign we get assigned." She grinned as she said it, but her eyes lingered on the napkin. "Is that your typical style?"

YOU CAN'T SAVE WHAT ISN'T THERE

"Most of the time when I'm doing it for myself. When the big round style was in vogue, I could do that, too." He coughed. "I read a lot of comics as a kid, and I learned from them, at first."

"I need versatility."

"And Cal's got *that*," Jason said. He shifted in his seat, focusing on Cal. "You're having fun, right?"

"Of course I am."

Jason inclined his head to the left and right. Lower, he said, "These are good people, I told you. I wouldn't hang out with them if they weren't."

"As long as Greg wasn't here. Gotta be honest, he reminded me of every frat brother we used to make fun of."

Jason laughed, hard, leaning over his tumbler glass. "Oh shit, you're *right*. Fuck." Snorting, he added. "We still crashed their parties, though."

"It was free beer if you could duck the cover charge."

Jason held up his drink, barely a whisper of brown liquor at the bottom. "Drink to *that*." He polished off the bourbon, then leaned in again, conspiratorially. "They didn't lowball you, did they? I know you were in a tight spot, but I didn't know what you made...*before*, and..."

Cal waved him off. "It was good. I accepted it right after I got off the phone with you. I go in on Monday."

Jason's grin seemed like it wanted to keep widening until the two ends met around the back of his head and toppled it off his neck. "That's fucking *great*, man. I'm *so* fucking happy for you. Sincerely."

"I'm happy, too." He finished off his beer in two big swallows, then coughed. In his mind's eye, he saw two images—the

45

rough sketches of the never-done graphic novel, and the picture of Elise's headstone Maggie had sent. His stomach burbled again, but it wasn't nausea this time, but a simmering...*some-thing*, and Cal felt his good feelings start to burn away, revealing that dark core beneath. That was the thing with loss when life—not a particular person's life, just life in general—kept boogying along; that dark core, that inability to conceptualize *forever*, stayed stubbornly put, reminding you of the hollow-ness of your minor, day-to-day triumphs. Who gave a shit, this dark core seemed to say, about a new job or a great haircut when the reality of tomorrow (and the next day and the next week and the next month) was such an impossibility? How stupid and petty were you to feel *good* about those things?

I should've gone to therapy, Cal thought, and that dark core seemed to sniff, *Shoulda, woulda, coulda. Elise is still dead at the end of it.*

Some of this must've shown on his face because Jason said, too loudly in Cal's ear and with a jubilance that sud-denly sounded forced to him, "Few more drinks, and we'll be willing to go steal some of those Bird scooters that col-lege kids rent to putter around the city." He clapped Cal's shoulder briskly—it felt like his old college friend was trying to roust him—and gestured at Cal's bottle with his tumbler glass. "Want another? My turn to buy."

Get it the fuck together, Cal told himself. *This is a cel-ebration, not a wake.* "*One* more. I don't have the balance for scooter-theft, my good bitch."

Jason slid off his seat. "We'll just see about *that*, motherfucker."

YOU CAN'T SAVE WHAT ISN'T THERE

Cal watched Jason merge with the crowd at the bar, hailing the occasional person he recognized—a real *Cheers* moment, Cal thought. Their colleagues drifted into their own conversations, leaving Cal in a bubble between the two sides.

He took a deep breath through his nose, then another. A part of him felt like he was trying to paper over that dark core, and maybe he was—for the time being. Today had been an authentically good, although categorically weird in places, good day.

His eyes dropped to his drawing. *It settled me*, he thought. *Art always settled you, you idiot*, the interior voice replied.

But not so literally. *I've also never worn a suit that I couldn't take off,* he thought, then jerked as felt a pin prick the back of his arm.

The streetlamps dazzled with astigmatism when Cal stepped outside a few hours later. The bar crowd had shifted, and a warm wave of hectic conversation followed him out, punctuated with the sounds of the sports matches from the televisions, now with volume on at ear-shattering levels.

Cal buttoned his coat. This patch of Wood Street, connecting to the main north-south thoroughfare of the Boulevard of the Alleys behind him with Liberty Avenue a few blocks further on, was wedged between Point Park college and government buildings, acting as a neutral ground of restaurants and bars for the diverse clientele. Pizzeria and Chinese restaurant signs jutted from brick facades, spaced between niche cafes and boho shops. Food smells mingled with the general grimy cold of city air currents. It wasn't as bad as the more industrial parts of the city, like the Bentley District, but you could still smell the metals of old factories, the ghosts of the old mills now decades dead—a tangy, hot-metal edge to the wind.

Cal rooted around the sketched-on napkin for his key fob. He'd debated calling an Uber or a Lyft for the back-and-forth, not knowing how his body would react to alcohol after taking an extended break without it, but his finances were precarious enough as it is. He drove, and made sure to sip, and he felt as sober now as he had when he arrived.

You say that, the interior voice remarked, *but I bet that fuckhead Franklin felt the same way just before he plowed into the school's turnaround.*

He felt a prick against the side of his neck, under his shirt collar, but he barely twitched. Goddamn, he thought as he made his way down the block, I'm getting used to it. He pulled out his keys...then the napkin, as well. Drawing it had made him feel better. His body had begun reacting to a change in the suit, but drawing had stopped it. What the hell did it mean? Now that he was away from the distraction of...not friends exactly, since he'd only known Jason in the group, but *being social*...the question lingered. A part of him, even with acknowledging the insanity of the afternoon, couldn't quite believe any of this. His brain could not properly contextualize it, but it seemed impossible to completely ignore it, and how in the fuck was he supposed to *sleep* in a suit? Every second brought up another question of the sheer *impracticality* of his insane situation. Was he supposed to *live* in his suit, randomly getting pricked by what felt like tailoring needles and only feel better when he was drawing? It would get filthy, *he* would get filthy, and his nerves, calm as they were now, would have a field day. Who or what could've dreamed up something like that?

His interior voice started to say, *A child—*, as he turned the corner down the side-street, and immediately shoulder-checked a person coming the opposite way.

Cal's hand clenched the napkin into a tight ball as he tried to keep his balance. The other man stumbled into the corner building's wall, arms flailing.

"Jesus," Cal said, catching his center of gravity. He pocketed the napkin. "You alright?"

The other man—bulky, a few inches shorter than Cal— splayed his hands against the wall and pushed himself off. He weaved more than he should've, head lowered, a boxer two rounds in and about to fall. "The fuck's wrong with you, man? Not see where you were going?"

"You weren't, either, dickhead," Cal's mouth snapped off, and barely noticed the fresh prick in the center of his chest. He looked around. The power suit crowd of the day had been replaced by college students and below-the-social-radar people, drifting into and out of the places still open—those bars and restaurants. The two of them had this patch of sidewalk to themselves.

The man raised his head, a shadowed, scuffy face and beady, glaring eyes, too old to be an undergrad, but younger than Cal. He looked familiar in that way people do in a small city, where many families stayed and mingled for generations, did. "You think you're better than me?"

"The fuck are you babbling about, asshole?" Cal asked. He felt an old tightening across his shoulders. The guy was drunk, it was obvious even if Cal hadn't smelled the astringent scent of vodka permeating from the guy's skin. Still, he felt his heart take on a percussive marching-beat in his chest, radiating out and down his arms. It'd been a while since he'd felt *that*.

The guy staggered forward a step. "The fuck you'd call me?"

Cal's legs pushed him forward, seemingly of their own will. "An asshole. The truth bother you?"

The guy grunted, showing a glimpse of teeth, and the idea of hearing those teeth crack and shattered suddenly seemed like it would sound positively musical to Cal.

What are you doing?—the interior voice asked, but it was faint, easy to ignore. Adrenaline seeped into his system, turning his veins and nerves into high-speed rails. The skin along the backs of his arms prickled, not with needles now, but like he'd been infested by ants with a purpose.

"Talking shit, man," the guy said. "You're talking shit."

Cal's mouth continued acting of its own accord. "You *are* a piece of shit, so we got something in common, then."

The guy swung, a haymaker telegraphed like a neon sign in darkness, and Cal sidestepped easily. The guy staggered, his center-of-gravity in his fist, stumbling towards the curb. Cal raised his foot and pistoned it against the small of the guy's back. He went flying, tumbling into the street hard.

YOU CAN'T SAVE WHAT ISN'T THERE

"Go the fuck home, you stupid drunk," Cal told him. His body vibrated with unspent energy, the sensation of ants crawling all over him now...but it didn't feel bad. Not at all. He hadn't felt this good since waking up to find he'd drawn those pages.

The guy turned himself around, and his expression, dramatically shadowed by a streetlamp, was a mixture of surprise and dumb, vapid rage, but Cal recoiled, staggering back a step.

The man looked familiar because it was the drunk, the guy, that fuckhead Franklin, the monster that had set this whole thing, *this whole thing*, in motion by blowing a stop sign during a day drunk.

Cal blinked—and, no, it *wasn't* the same guy, it could never have been, but he *almost* looked like him, so close they could've been cousins. And it didn't seem to matter—his body vibrated with the urge, the *need*, to launch himself at the guy.

"*Motherfucker!*" the drunk yelled, propelling himself at Cal. Cal reached out, almost casually, with hands that seemed longer and bigger and somehow *darker* in the street-light, like he'd dumped them into a vat of black ink, and grabbed the drunk's shoulders, stopping the guy's momentum easily. With a snarl that didn't sound the least bit human, the least bit like *himself*, he pivoted at the waist and threw the guy against the wall like a sack of laundry.

Cal stomped over to him, hands clenching and unclench-ing, his skin tingling and tingling and tingling. In the back of his mind, the thought *not the same not the same* went in a circle, but it didn't matter. He bent, again picking up the guy as if he were nothing but a pillow, and slammed him face first into the wall. The *crack* was loud, the splash of blood made dark against the brick.

He did it again, and again, seething air through clenched teeth. By the fourth time, the drunk was completely boneless, his face a mask of blood, and Cal dropped him.

He looked down at his hands. For the briefest second, they *were* larger, they *were* black, the fingers long and spidery, topped with conical claws that gleamed like onyx in the light. He squawked, and his hands were normal again, but shaking with adrenaline. He saw a gossamer of blood thread its way out from under the cuff of his shirt, as if he'd cut his arm inside his shirt.

The drunk gave a throaty groan, and Cal looked around wildly. *What the fuck just happened?* Confusion filled him as surely and completely as the adrenaline had an instant before.

Cal bolted.

Delayed reaction held off on the barely-remembered drive home, but set its teeth into the soft lengths of his nerves when he shut his apartment door behind him.

He went down onto his hands and knees in the entryway. His insides became unglued and sloshed around as he prostrated, his lips peeled back from chattering teeth. He seethed out hot patches of air against the scuffed hardwood, buffeting his suddenly chilled cheeks.

YOU CAN'T SAVE WHAT ISN'T THERE

Cal reared back, hugging his midsection, the damned suit whispering against his skin, under his hands—his *normal* hands.

"The fuck," he muttered. "What the fuck, what the *fuck*—"

Every inch of his skin creeped and crawled, legions of ants underneath, but this time it was intolerable, pulling apart his thoughts like wet paper. Cal tore at his sides, his shoulders, his arms, until the pain of friction lessened the itch. Two spots on his brow burned with irritation, the way clammy sweat did against dry skin, and he dug at them with his nails, barking with satisfaction.

He goggled at his living room as he dug at himself, dark and built in blocks of shadows, the drawings highlighted by the television's glow.

Can't take off the suit, can only feel better with drawing—
(you're doing it daddy!)

Cal keened, seeing Elise from his dream, her face side-lit by the sun in a window that didn't get sunlight in reality.

(keep making good choices)

And then he saw the drunk, the asshole he'd thought for an instant had been the monster that had started all of this, and, oh my god, how *good* it felt to hurt him, to *make him* feel even just a *fraction* of how Cal felt every second of every day.

But it *hadn't been* Mr. Scott Franklin, driving on a suspended license, pleading guilty to manslaughter to avoid a murder-two rap. Cal had *known* this, but it *hadn't mattered*, and it had felt *good*. How much better would it have felt *had* it been Franklin? All of them, actually—every single person he held responsible for what had happened?

He thought of his hands, extending from the oh-so-perfect half-inch of dress shirt as monstrous, oversized claws of ebony and onyx. He keened again, a tea kettle through his grinding teeth, and his scrambling fingers found the labels of his jacket, the buttons of his shirt. He looked through eyes shrink-wrapped in tears at the highlighted coffee table. He hadn't drawn that well in *years*, but it fucking *hurt*.

"This fucking *suit*—" Cal choked out, and wrenched his shirt open. Buttons popped and flew as pain chainsawed into his chest, a whirling dervish of sharp, pointed teeth against weak flesh and fragile bone. Cal shrieked, his vision blackening rapidly, but not before he saw blood fly, a ruby-crimson spray into the air.

Cal fell forward, slamming hard into a floor that felt as soft as a feather mattress.

Elise, over his shoulder, the room still bathed in that mellow-yellow sunlight, the monstrosity in the suit still bathed in the duck-neck lamp: "You don't have to do it this way, Daddy. You have a choice."

He's penciling the monster, adding texture and dimension, less Bernie Wrightson and more Klaus Janson, now, still comic book. The monster kneels in his perfect suit, head lowered and spiral horns arcing high above his head. His eyes are red—Cal uses a simple Crayola color pencil for this—and blood drips out from under the wrists of his suit shirt. A little ways away, within snatching distance but more foregrounded than the monstrosity, Cal's sketched a small, rough humanoid outline silhouetted in a glow constructed of feather-light pencil strokes. In the dream, he finds himself annoyed that he doesn't have the right shade of light blue for the illumination.

"You're making art, Daddy," Elise says, unseen but felt, and is she wearing that dress again? Is her tangle of brunette curls turned into mahogany fire in the sunlight? He wants to turn around to see, but he can't. He has to draw...this thing. His hands won't stop.

"The art will save you," Elise says, and she sounds almost sad, like she knows this is the truth, but that it also won't matter. "You don't have to let this happen."

And Cal speaks, but it's not his voice, not the one he's heard all his life, but something thick and grinding and guttural. On some level, his interior voice, now completely subsumed within his mind, tells him that this is the voice of pain and anger and loss mixed.

"But it won't stop hurting," he tells his daughter in his new monster voice.

Before she can reply, his vision goes black—

—and he's wedged between the couch and coffee table again, the light of the television, now on the late-late show, washing coldly over him.

He raised his head. His face was puffy from crying, his arms aching from hugging his knees to his chest.

"Oh god," he muttered, swallowing. His cheeks were wet, but drying, like he'd been sobbing hard, but had stopped at some point without cleaning himself up.

He looked down at himself. The suit was perfect again, every button in place, not a stain on it. He looked from it to the apartment entryway. Smeared blood on the hardwood, tacky and turning maroon, more dotting and dribbled on the walls around it.

"It was real," he said. He awkwardly got himself up from his wedged position, staggering over to the mess. His mind turned to the bottle of cleaner under the kitchenette sink, an old T-shirt rag, it looked like a murder had happened there. Couldn't leave it, Jesus, think of the security deposit.

Cal leaned against the archway between living space and entryway, hands going to his chest as he stared down at the mess. His skin was whole, not even tender. And no itchy, pricking sensation.

Trapped. The word floated up from the blackness at the bottom of his mind like the last air bubble of a drowning victim. He was impossibly trapped in this impossible suit. It let him do things, like toss people as if they were bundles of paper, and—

He turned slowly, back to the pages on the coffee table. From the distance, the papers looked covered with blobs of gray and black.

"What have I done now?" he breathed. He scooped up the papers and dropped onto the couch itself, using the light of the television to see. He shuffled through the pages drawn before, finally finding the new ones.

Larger panels on the first new page, the Norm Breyfogle angles more extreme. Focus over Elise's shoulder, showing the car lane emptying, giving her (and the viewer) the sight-lines of an old Toyota ripping through the T-intersection—the back of a stop sign prominent, meant to be seen—beyond the roundabout, turning in a way that indicated it might've flipped with just a little more momentum or a harder twist of the wheel—

(and, oh, how Cal wished that had been the case, muscles in his cheeks twitching, and shifted absently against the fresh pinprick in his back)

—the driver beyond the windshield a hulking shape, each panel showing the Toyota looming larger and larger in the foreground, the "camera" never leaving Elise's shoulder, until, finally, a square box of black, drawn so harshly the paper was dimpled inward, about to tear.

"Fuck," Cal said, his voice thick and phlegmy, and flipped to the next page.

Another too-black panel, and then the viewer was back at the heaven angle, high above the front of the school, Franklin's car buried in the top left corner, indicating there was horror beyond it. Figures like army men scattered around, frozen.

The image held, almost identical for three separate panels, and then a new vehicle entered the car lane, bottom right, and Cal's hand had been meticulous in making sure it came across for what it was: a Subaru Forrester, shaded to indicate color, but Cal saw olive green in his mind's eye. Hadn't it been parked in the driveway of Maggie's home whenever he picked up Elise on the weekends?

The perspective held with the driver getting out of the car, another army man, before switching to a view from below, looking up. It was no longer over the shoulder, but Cal (and the viewer) knew whose perspective it was, and weight grew in Cal's chest as his eyes went from panel to panel, the new driver growing larger and more distinct as they left the car behind and approached. The second to last panel went from margin to margin, widescreen, the driver like a gunslinger in one-half of a duel: Dennis. His face is a mask of shock, broad shoulders slumped and hands limp at his sides, as the sun lit off the bristles of his buzzcut.

Between this panel and the identically-shaped but another too-black panel beneath, Cal had written out *AAAAWHOAWHOAWHOAWHOAWHOAWHOA*. The emergency sirens, too late to do anything. Like Dennis.

Cal sniffed, pressure blocking out his sinuses. "Oh fuck, you motherfucker. You fuck."

The last page was only half-filled, the top row of three panels all too-black again, the second row that bizarre stained-glass design he'd sketched on the cover, each panel pulling back as the design seemed to rotate, the final panel again showing the perspective of over Elise's shoulder—her shoulder, side of her neck and distinct curls taking up the left edge.

Cal let the papers fall into his lap, leaden chest hitching. "You fucking bastards," he whispered. "Should've been you, not her. Should've done your fucking jobs."

YOU CAN'T SAVE WHAT ISN'T THERE

He rolled his hands into fists. In the dim light, they were ashen and large, the fingers seemingly longer.

He swallowed convulsively, trying to get himself under control, but all he saw in his mind's eye was the faces of the guilty in the aftermath—Flaherty's husband, flushed and hectic, unable to admit his wife was just as guilty as Franklin, only of negligence; Franklin himself, at the sentencing, accepting the plea agreement of manslaughter and partial-time-served, Cal had only gotten a brief glimpse of that vapid evil because Cal had bellowed in the courtroom, had to be dragged out by bailiffs; Dennis, blank at the funeral, idiotically shocked that not being on time had ended so horrendously.

Cal hissed, and it sounded like a furnace letting off steam. There were others, of course—the emergency vehicles who'd dawdled; the prosecutors who wanted to avoid the trial; the school officials who didn't think they had to change their pickup policy, letting kids roam around within striking distance of a line of two-ton hulks of rolling steel and glass.

"Elise had been *good*," he breathed. *"She'd held that bitch's hand."* But it'd been like holding the hand of someone at the edge of a fatal, crumbling cliff, hadn't it?

(you don't have to let this happen)

Elise's voice, whispered into his ear, in his mind, in his dream, and Cal shook, every muscle beneath this damned suit taut and thrumming with the same energy that had tossed that stupid drunk into the wall. Pinpricks, like the strings of indecisive bees, across his chest.

"But it won't stop *hurting*," he breathed, his eyes hard and dry and hot. He heard his voice saying to Jason, *I'm happy, too.*

The papers slid off his lap, puddled around his shining black shoes, and he looked down at his fists, shaking against his thighs, and, yes, the fingers did look longer, the hands themselves larger than he remembered, the skin darker in the dim light, a bracelet of bright white from the immaculate half-inch of shirt shooting from the cuff.

Cal snarled down at them, and his voice was thick and deep and roiling, and he didn't even hear what could've been a disappointed sigh.

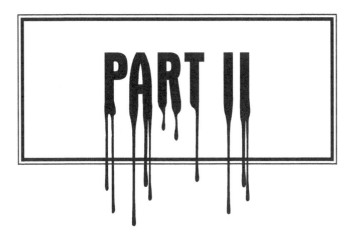

he line rang long enough that Cal feared it'd go to voice mail, but then, just before he would've tried fumbling his way through a message that wouldn't arouse suspicion, he heard a click, and a gruff, disoriented male voice said, "Hello? Yes?"

"Mr. Thompson?" he asked, hearing how gravelly his voice was.

"Yes?" The tone not disoriented but suspicious now. A telemarketer, Thompson might've been thinking. Cal could imagine the prosecutor's young, camera-ready face, ready to be angry, probably thinking, *These bastards don't even take the weekends off.*

He shouldn't have taken the weekends off, Cal thought. *Should've wanted to go to trial, the son of a bitch.*

"It's Cal Matheson," he said. "I apologize for calling so early, and on a Saturday, no less—"

"Mr. Matheson," Thompson said, his voice slowing.

"You remember me?"

"Of course, Mr. Matheson," Thompson said. "I always remember the people we try to help."

Such help, Cal thought, and his grip tightened on his phone until the protective case crinkled. A pinprick against his forearm.

"What can I do for you?" Thompson asked.

Cal cleared his throat. It sounded like water splashing against river-smooth rocks to his ears. "I was talking to my ex-wife, and she'd brought up Scott Franklin. Worrying, I mean. About when he went free, and—" He trailed off, trying to make it sound like he was fumbling through the words.

Thompson jumped in, as Cal had wanted. "I understand, Mr. Matheson. I really do, but neither you nor your ex-wife have anything left to fear—"

Because our child's already dead, Cal thought, but said, "It's not for us, I mean, but—" Again that pause, as if trying to find the right phrase, but another baited hook.

"You and your ex-wife feared him being in a similar situation to what led to the tragedy with your child," Thompson finished.

Tragedy's a word for it, sure. Cal's teeth ground against each other. "Pretty much. We couldn't remember the details of his sentencing, and I told her what I remembered—time in prison, plus monitoring—but when we got off the phone, *I* started to wonder if I had it right, and—"

"How did you get my personal number, Mr. Matheson?" Thompson asked. He said it with, in Cal's ears, an almost courtroom flair, the kind of tone and pitch one expected to hear on drama shows when the hotshot attorney knew he was about to force a witness to reveal an uncomfortable truth.

But apparently this junior-junior-what-the-fuck-ever assistant D.A.'s memory *wasn't* as great as he'd thought. "You'd given it to us, Mr. Thompson. On your business card, before the arraignment." *When you and your boss offered such a sweetheart fucking deal to a child killer,* he didn't add.

"Oh," Thompson replied. He sounded almost deflated, and Cal's dry lips spread in a grin.

Cal gave it a beat, then said, "Anyway, Scott Franklin's sentencing...?"

"Next time you talk to your ex-wife, Mr. Matheson," Thompson said, "please reassure her: Scott Franklin is never going to have any of the ingredients needed to repeat what happened. He spent eight months behind bars and is now on strictly supervised house-arrest, living with a brother or some relative near the Bentley District, far from any school, for the foreseeable future. We made sure of that."

I'm sure you did, Cal thought, leaning forward, driving his smartphone against his ear.

"He's banned from having a driver's license," Thompson continued, "and must meet very-strict pop-up inspections from the state or else he goes away again." He paused. "I'm just more sorry than you can know that it took the loss of a child to finally put a stop to that man's actions."

Not your *child, but a* child, *you fucking politico coward,* Cal thought. *You have no idea what sorry is, but I could show you.* Cal's lips pulled back from his teeth, the dry skin cracking and sending little flares of pain.

"Anyway," Thompson said, "if you or your ex-wife ever have any questions, please don't hesitate to call the district attorney's office—"

"Of course, and I'm sorry for calling you on the weekend like this. It's just, it was rattling around in my head for a few days, and I worried—"

"I understand," he said, but he didn't. He couldn't. That was the problem, Cal discovered; everyone *said* they "understood", but who did, really? Even those who'd lost someone themselves, could anyone really *know*, really *understand*? Pain and loss and grief were subjective, so tailor-made, as to make any kind of naming of it meaningless. Hearing "I understand" from those who'd also lost someone—whether due to age, illness, or some other catastrophe—made Cal cringe, feel strangely brittle. Hearing it from some polished, opportunistic bastard like Thompson made the statement vulgar. Obscene.

"Thank you, Mr. Thompson," Cal said. "Have a good rest of your morning." He clicked off before Thompson could reply, tossed his phone onto the coffee table.

He sat back. Morning light, gray as always, fell through the room's sole window, highlighting the dust motes kicked up by tossing the phone. *He's going to be suspicious now,* the interior voice said. *He might organize a check-in on that fuckhead today or tomorrow just because of this.*

Cal waved a gray hand. "Doesn't matter. Not really." He saw his hand and turned it towards him. The nails were longer, a charcoal gray. "And if he gets in my way...well, he's partly responsible for all this, too."

YOU CAN'T SAVE WHAT ISN'T THERE

A sigh whispered past his right ear, and Cal spun around, damned suit rustling. Nothing there, of course. He heard his coffee maker burbling to itself.

(you don't have to do this daddy)

"You think that, but you're wrong, sweetie. I have to stop the hurting. I have to make it right."

For who, though? the interior voice asked.

He leaned forward to pick his phone back up from atop the pages, the rough cover on top because it was the least-painful image in the stack. *Elise Matheson and Her Incredible Interdimensional Journey.* A working title, but it *did* work. His eyes lingered over his sketch of her. He'd gotten her hair right, that junior Medusa snarl of curls. His eyes grew hot.

(the art will save you—you don't have to let this happen)

Cal swallowed the lump in his throat. For a brief moment, where even the stupid sounds of the television seemed to halt and the room seemed to lighten, he looked at the cover, and a part of him thought, yes, he could focus on the art. The art, which had always been his salvation, his safe harbor, when life would take a left turn into the shitstorm. His child was gone, his career was on life support, but he still had art, and it'd already started working its magic again—didn't he have work on Monday? He could do it, as well as do the story he'd dreamed-up during that lone, falsely-bright week some months ago. He might've been an atheist, but there was no dogma in imagination, and no lack of faith. He could imagine what happened after and be hopeful, be a loving father, one last time. The drawings he'd done, they were premiere pages, sure, but he could get the standard size, make samples to start pitching.

He could move on, grow from this, build a life that would've made Elise happy if she'd been around to see it. It was all *right there,* beneath those rough pages, some of the best art he'd ever done, or probably would ever do. It *could* save him, and Elise *would* be happy, wherever she was.

A last chance, the interior voice said, and Cal looked at his hand, holding the phone a few inches above the page, how dark and wrinkled it already was, the nails sharpening.

"Elise can't be happy," he said with his rough voice. "Elise is dead."

The room dimmed, he heard the paid-for audience of an early-morning infomercial clap and applaud, and he leaned back in his chair, holding the phone to his midsection. A painful weight, like the sharpened edge of a stone, dug into his heart. His skin itched beneath the suit, those focused ants marching. He didn't know what that meant and didn't care—not like he could do anything about it, anyway. His eyes stayed on the art and saw it for what it was—an artifact. Something dusky and old, unearthed. Dead.

"It never stops hurting," he said. He heard a sigh again, but he didn't turn around. He blinked his hot eyes once, twice, then powered up his phone, opened his browser, and went to the White Pages.

There were a dozen Franklins in Hathaway and the out-lying neighborhoods, but only one Franken, Emory, lived in the Bentley District, on 11th Street. An industrial wasteland that, for decades before the slow historical rewriting of gentrification, had seemed like a monument to the city's former blue-collar glory, the Bentley District hugged the eastern edge of the city's Bachman River. The main thoroughfare, Pitt Avenue, ran straight down the middle, with downtown at one end and the college neighborhoods of Oakdale and Squirrel Hill on the other.

Cal found the address easily enough, a corner rowhouse on 11th and Baltimore Street. Three steps to the door, narrow in width, two floors, old blinds covered the lone window to the left of the door, signaling that a younger person lived there (the rest of the occupied houses all had aged, frilly curtains, owned by older folks who'd withstood the continuous decline of the area and hoped to survive the superficial revival). No car parked out front, but that didn't tell anything—the curb was painted yellow, a flaking fire hydrant standing guard.

He drove past, turning off onto Baltimore, than did a three-pointer in the mouth of an alley so he could park along the opposite curb, the postage stamp backyard of the Franklin house, marked off by a waist-high chainlink fence, visible out his driver's side window. He killed the engine.

The street was dead, the few cars and trucks parked along the curb were antique by comparison to his Honda, their paintjobs faded and windows thin and becoming milky with age. Even with the Honda's windows rolled up, the chill seeped in, carrying the dominant scent of the Bentley District, the ghost smell of dead earth and old metal and faded oil. No one walked the littered curbs. The morning was a gloomy no-color. The windows of the occupied homes were covered thoroughly, as if to shun the degradation of the formerly working-class neighborhood. The windows of the emptied houses, about half of what he could see from his vantage point, stared back at Cal with blank idiot eyes.

He looked down at his changing hands, but didn't acknowledge the reality of them. He felt the ants marching across his skin, but he had to consciously think to do so. He glanced at his eyes in the rearview mirror. They were deeply bloodshot, the blues like sapphire stones embedded in ripe cherries.

Don't, a little girl's voice sighed from behind him, and Cal spun around, but the backseat was empty. Of course.

Cal faced front again. While the wild hope had been that the fuckhead would be out and about, walking free while Cal's daughter's corpse rotted, that wasn't likely, given the house arrest. The fuckhead would be hiding in his brother's house, on time he didn't deserve, waiting until he was *really* free again. He probably couldn't walk to the corner store, though, oh, the humanity.

Cal turned it over in his mind. Thompson might've been spooked, or it might've been Cal's own paranoia, but... He looked at himself. He was wearing the suit. He looked so out of place in this place, and wouldn't the people meant to be checking up on Franklin be dressed professionally, too? Probably. Even if not, it wouldn't matter in the end.

What about your eyes? the interior voice asked. *Your skin? Your hands, Cal? You think the oddness of a* suit *in the Bentley District is going to paper that over?*

He glanced at his hellishly red eyes again. "It doesn't matter." He got out of the car, the *thunk* of the door closing loud. He looked around, making sure all those curtains in all those occupied houses *were* buttoned up tight, and—

The metallic scream of metal hinges, and Cal whirled around to see the man of the hour, Scott Franklin, dumpy and bedraggled in an oversized Pittsburgh Penguins hoodie and baggy sweats, stepped down the back steps, letting the screen door slam shut behind him. He fumbled around in the hoodie's kangaroo pocket, producing a crumpled pack of cigarettes and lighter.

Cal's entire body became one flexed muscle. His vision narrowed to just the sight of the man, last seen from the back when Cal had sat in the courtroom's audience. He was moving before he was aware his legs were working, as if the street were a conveyer belt. He stepped up onto the sidewalk, only hearing the heavy thump of his pulse in his ears, only feeling the growing heat on the itchy skin beneath his suit. He saw Franklin raise his head to send a plume of exhaled smoke into the air, but didn't *really* see him. Instead, his mind's eye took over, showing him the dumpy fuck in the orange jumpsuit, showing him Elise in her checked dress with the wide straps in the open casket, showing him the ruined landscaping the fuck's car had plowed through and the smear of blood against the sandy wall of the elementary school building. Whose blood had it been? Elise's or the teacher's?

He flicked aside the fence's latch with a hand that might've been on another planet, metal scraping metal, and Scott Franklin spun around, mealy mouth dropping open. The man needed a shave, his clammy-looking jowls bristling with gray and brown hairs.

"The fuck—" Scott Franklin said, his voice nasally and clogged. His face was the same vapid evil Cal had seen in the courtroom, the piggish anger at being punished for being caught, an overgrown child cosplaying as an adult, the monster who had taken Cal's child and didn't understand why anyone would hate him.

"Fuckhead," Cal growled.

He stood between Franklin and the assumed-safety of the house, but Franklin broke right, lit cigarette and lighter tumbling out of his grasp. Cal's hand flashed out, catching Franklin in the shoulder, sending the bigger man into the wall with a solid *thud*. Franklin's feet flew out from under him, dropping him to the concrete pavers.

Whose blood, whose blood—It chanted through Cal's head.

Cal towered over him, every itchy inch of him warm, every part of him thrumming with energy. He wanted to say something, to tell this fuckhead what he'd done, the pain he'd caused, the lives he ruined, but another part of him, the majority, didn't see the point.

Franklin goggled up at him, his face a mask of fear, but he had no right to that feeling. You fear when you think something is about to go wrong in ways you can't predict. This fuckhead had earned it.

Scott Franklin hadn't earned the right to be afraid.

Cal bent forward, inhuman hands grasping the sides of Franklin's head, and yanked the man forward. Franklin came easily, as if he weighed nothing at all, and it was like the drunk the night before, the one Cal had *thought* had been

YOU CAN'T SAVE WHAT ISN'T THERE

this fuckhead, but now it was better, because Franklin was finally and completely in his grasp. Franklin mewled up at him, and Cal snarled down into that frightened face.

Cal shoved Franklin's head against the house's back wall, the meaty, wet *crack* forcing a bark of satisfaction from him. Franklin's eyes rolled, dazed. Cal yanked him forward and shoved him again—another meaty *crack*, and now a blood smear coated the brick.

(whose blood whose blood)

He did it over and over, until his darkening hands were coated in blood, until Franklin's limp legs stopped drummed along the concrete pavers, until Cal's arms grew tired. Cal's mind went away, and it felt like it took a while, but really only lasted a few seconds in the world of time beyond Cal's narrowed focus.

With a final grunt, Cal drove the man's head into the wall and felt the change in the skull shape beneath his callused palms, the sudden yielding quality in the structure. He let go, and Scott Franklin slumped, his eyes bleeding and glazed, bulging in two different directions from dark craters. More blood trickled from his ears. His unkempt hair had hills and valleys. The wall behind him looked like it'd been the bullseye for a volley of water balloons filled with red paint.

(whose blood whose blood)

Cal stepped back. He felt heavy weight on his chest, but for the first time in a long time, it didn't hurt. Instead, the heaviness reminded him of the way one felt when they completed a hard but necessary physical task.

Human thought—and a dim part of him noted that it was strange to think of it that way—trickled back in: *The first one. The first.*

Metal hinges screamed again, and Cal spun to see a reedy younger man in Buddy Holly glasses and a faded novelty t-shirt fly out the back door, tight fists at the end of narrow arms. "Scott, goddammit, the fuck are you—"

He froze as he took in Cal and the Franklin's corpse. "What the fuck?" he said on a rushed exhale of air.

"You must be the brother," Cal remarked, and his voice was like crushing gravel. He swiped at the younger man, and his nails, longer now, darker, caught in the side of the man's throat. The momentum yanked Cal forward, but he held onto his balance as the Franklin brother lost his own footing, gagging at the sudden rush of blood into his mouth.

Cal grunted, bending forward to grip the man's throat completely, his thumbnail piercing the other side. Fresh hot blood coated his hand. He pulled, and the man's throat came apart like taffy, splashing more blood onto the concrete. Cal straightened, shaking loose bits of flesh free off his fingers, droplets spattering. The younger Franklin sunfished on the ground, hands pawing at nothing, his Buddy Holly glasses falling off and cracking on the cement.

Cal waited until the man went still with a final shiver of one sneaker, then stepped over the body and left the backyard. All of the curtained windows still separated their occupants from the world outside.

He approached the car and, for a moment, saw a small, humanoid shape behind the driver's seat. He flashed onto the thing he'd been drawing in his dream, and what felt like a blanket of nails swaddled him. He staggered and spasmed in the street, holding onto his balance through miracle and little else.

He didn't have the time to scream before the sensation left, like something within his nerves had flicked a switch. He straightened gingerly, waiting for the feeling to return. When it didn't, he got into the car.

In the rearview mirror, the blue of his eyes seemed to be retreating from the red, and his skin was the color of old tombstones except for two irritated patches to either side of his widow's peak, like abnormally large pimples that refused to come to a head.

He looked away and started the engine. It didn't matter. Everything about this was insane, really, from an impossible-to-remove-suit on down, so why not this, as well? It had benefits, after all.

He glanced into the backyard and thought you couldn't really tell what you were looking at from this distance. The backstairs blocked the view of Scott Franklin's resting place, and the view of the younger Franklin was obscured by blue garbage cans—only the sneakers were visible.

Cal waited to see if guilt or regret or *something* would fill him, but nothing did, just that tired job-well-done sensation. This had been right. His own heart told him so.

He drove away, hands that were more clawlike now navigating the steering wheel.

The memorial Elise's school had cobbled together two weeks after the accident had been a sad affair, Cal had thought, even just by looking at the mailed invitation addressed to THE FAMILIES OF REGINALD FIELDING ELEMENTARY. The desperate actions of an institution trying to show compassion so you'd be too distracted to sue. He hadn't planned on going, let the school officials writhe in worry that he *would* sue, but Maggie had convinced him.

"Everyone liked Elise," she said over the phone, one of the few times she felt compelled to call instead of text. "They're going to want to offer their condolences, and you wanted to keep the funeral private."

"I don't want their fucking condolences, Maggie," he'd said, pacing his old condo, which had been twice the size of his apartment.

"It's not about you, Cal," Maggie had replied. "It's about *Elise*, dammit."

He'd heard her voice, then, how her voice had *sounded*—tight, but on the edge, the way she always sounded when she was about to cry.

"Okay, okay—sorry." He'd closed his eyes, squeezed them tight until arcs of light had sketched behind his lids. "Okay, Maggie. Okay. I get it."

"Do you?" she'd asked and just twist the knife in, already. She said it in the tone she used to use when they were winding up for one of their *real* fights, the ones that sounded like discussions if you only heard the volume and speed with which they spoke.

YOU CAN'T SAVE WHAT ISN'T THERE

"Yeah, I do." He sighed. "We'll do the united front thing, okay?" He paused. "Is Dennis—"

"He's going, Cal," she'd cut him off. "He was an active part of Elise's life, too."

Weariness had filled him like water filling a tall glass. "All right. I'll see you there."

"You will?" Still almost the tone of I-*will*-fight-you-on-this-Calvin.

"*Yes*. Jesus, Maggie."

"Okay, then." Slowly letting it go, like a dog loosening its grip on a forbidden item. "Thank you."

And the whole affair *had* been just as sad and pathetic and desperate as Cal had thought it'd be. The administration had staged the whole thing in the cafeteria-*cum*-auditorium—a wide, tiled space with cylindrical columns ringing the edges, facing a low, three-steps-up wooden stage. All the children's tables had been folded and shunted into a side hallway beside it, letting the adults and their children mill about in the central space, hands full of bitter coffee or juice or store-bought snacks from long folding tables shoved against the doorways leading to the lunch line. Up on the stage, large blowups of Elise's spring portrait and Flaherty's faculty picture rested on easels, next to small tables with wide books where people "could write remembrances," as the pudgy assistant principal had explained from the stage's bottom step, worrying his hands in front of his shiny blue suit as an older, more severe woman, the head principal, stood behind him like a monolith.

He'd almost squeaked when his raisin eyes had fallen on Cal, standing at the front of the group, but Cal had barely noticed him. His eyes had been locked on Elise's image. He'd never even had a chance to see the spring portraits. She was buried in the same dress, but in the picture she wore a blue headband that matched the dress, partially corralling her wild hair.

And he had stood there, staring at his daughter, feeling the rough edge of a stone not just *press* but rub vigorously against his chest, forcing him to almost hunch over, as if hugging the rock. He wanted to lie down, right on the floor, but that wouldn't have removed the pressure, of course. Fine, then—drive him into the ground, through the ground, pulverize him. Jesus Christ, did these fuckheads really think any of *this* would help? The entire affair reminded him of those clouds of gnats that circled you when you were outdoors and sweating, how they distracted and irritated your thoughts.

He thought, later, that people might've recognized him— he and Elise had looked remarkably alike—and approached, but if they did, he had no idea what they said, or if he replied, or how. A part of him, the part that remembered a time in his life when he hadn't been Grieving Father™, hoped he hadn't been rude—they weren't to blame for what had happened. The rest of him didn't give a fuck. The attending families buzzed around him, but he was rooted to the spot, staring at Elise's photo and thinking how she'd died before he'd even been able to see it, before he and Maggie would've discussed what package to buy from Strawberry Bridge so they could divvy up the copies accordingly. Something as nonsensical as that bounced around his mind like the beads in maracas, leaving him unable to focus on anything else.

YOU CAN'T SAVE WHAT ISN'T THERE

Cal roused when Maggie and Dennis arrived through the cafeteria's side door—Maggie in the lead and standing out with her wild curly hair, Dennis looking, of course, like a hobo marveling at the interior of a mansion. They were dressed business casual—slacks and button-downs, as if, aside from Dennis's Neanderthal-seeing-a-smartphone expression, they'd stepped whole and breathing from one of the ad campaigns Cal had worked on. He could almost picture the mockup in his mind, which should've been impressive to him—he'd taken a leave from his firm the day Elise had died and hadn't visualized anything since—but wasn't. All he felt was a low-heat in his gut—Maggie had harangued him to come, and then hadn't bothered showing up until halfway through, and, at that moment, he didn't particularly give a fuck if she had the tell-tale signs he knew so well that she'd recently been crying.

He looked away instead of going to them—fuck that united front business. He spied the flop-sweat-attracting assistant principal, hiding in the overhang that gave way to the school's main hallway, speaking urgently to the main principal who nodded along almost imperceptibly. Kids, most not quite understanding what they were doing at school after hours, haunted the snack table or whined to their impatient parents to be let into the closed gym next to the cafeteria. Those children who *did* seem to understand clung to their own parents and looked at the portrait of their old teacher, eyes irritated and wet. He saw a few young men and woman, clustered together, that had to be school teachers. Teachers, Cal thought, had to be the only profession in the world where no matter how well put together they were, their entire beings exuded weariness and stress, even after hours.

The only person flying solo, like Cal, was a youngish man standing in the center of the room, and glaring at the portraits. He appeared a few inches shorter than Cal, but with the broader shoulders and oversized hands extending from his brownish-gray Carhartt jacket that telegraphed outdoor work. His blockhead was frosted with gray, but it looked new.

He caught Cal looking, glanced back at the portraits, and his eyes widened like a cartoon bull's that had just seen the color red. *Fuck*, Cal had time to think before the man was beside him, swinging one of those cinderblock fists, and Cal's head rocked up and back, black stars arcing in a shower across his vision.

Next, he was on his ass, pressed into one of the columns, while the man drove fist and fist into his face and chest, but the pain was instantly secondary as he realized not just that the man was shrieking, but what he was saying.

"Where the fuck were you?" the man cried. He *was* crying, full-on gushing-tears sobs that rained down on Cal's bleeding face. *"Why the fuck didn't you pick up your fucking kid? It's your fault! IT'S ALL YOUR FAULT!"*

He thinks I was the one who was late, Cal thought and suddenly the rage was there, like the man's accusation had been the right magic words to unlock the secret well within him. He stopped feeling the pain, but not in a numbing way—more, it *galvanized* him, like it was an electrical prod.

His vision grayed, and he came back to hands on his arms and shoulders, trying to yank him back. He and the man had switched places, and he was the one raining blows onto the other's face.

"*IT'S NOT MY FAULT!*" he bellowed, punching, trying to obliterate the man's teeth and nose the way the drunk driver had obliterated their loved ones. "*I WASN'T EVEN THERE!*" The crowd succeeded in pulling him off, and his vision spun, taking in the blood on the tiled floor, the shocked crowd ringing them, finally settling on Maggie and Dennis, twin expressions of shock.

Cal had jabbed a shaking, bloody finger at Dennis. "*IT'S HIS FUCKING FAULT! HIS FUCKING FAULT THAT MY CHILD IS DEAD! WHERE THE FUCK WERE YOU, DENNIS? WHERE THE FUCK WERE YOU!*"

The pullers dragged him to the side hallway where the lunch tables were folded, but not before seeing Maggie burst into tears, seeing Dennis lose twenty years on his face and become a small child suddenly in trouble, and he'd shrieked, "*GOOD! You should feel bad you motherfuckers—*"

—and Cal's smartphone was ringing.

Cal jerked in the driver's seat, parked and engine idling, with MAGGIE spelled out above the words ACCEPT and REJECT on the dashboard screen, and the default smartphone ringtone blaring from the speakers.

"The hell?" he growled. In his lap, he had a flyer, the kind of half-sheet of colored paper you sometimes found beneath your windshield wiper, and he'd drawn on the flipside, a rough sketch of a man, heavily shadowed to show the illumination coming from the front, where a three-steps-up stage had been erected with two blank portrait easels standing on it. The man's shoulders were slumped, hands dangling, while a homogenous humanoid crowd ringed the space around him. He held the pen awkwardly in a hand where the nails grew a half-inch from the fingertips, dull black, and the flesh had coarsened and darkened. But the marching ants were gone. His suit was still stained, but he felt no discomfort.

The dashboard let out the beep of a missed call, and then all he could hear was the engine. He looked around—he'd parked in the same large lot behind Elise's school he'd used the night of the memorial. It was empty aside from two identical dark minivans with the school district's logo on the doors and an older Lexus, parked closer to the cafeteria doors.

"Holy shit," Cal breathed. He'd been driving, trying to figure out how he would get to the asshole husband, and thinking of the last time he'd seen him, here at this school, but somehow his remembrance had become...well, more like a dream, and he'd come here, parked, and started drawing.

Like when you tried taking off the suit, his interior voice added, and Cal repelled the pen from his hand like it was something hot. It rolled off the dashboard. The drawing slid off his leg and between his feet in the footwell. The hairs on the back of his neck tingled, the way they did when someone else entered a room but you didn't see them yet.

Cal didn't feel alone.

"Elise?" he asked, feeling alternately completely ridiculous and not ridiculous at all. Was the idea of the ghost of his daughter any more ridiculous than this damned suit, or murdering the drunk driver and his brother, or how his entire body was changing? "Are you here, Elise?"

The phone rang again, and Cal jerked in his seat, top of his head brushing the ceiling, and he hissed as his sensitive skin rubbed against the tight, industrial fabric. He put a hand to his forehead, feeling the bumps from before, hot under his callused skin, and saw MAGGIE on the dashboard screen again. He jabbed a finger at ACCEPT, and said, "Yeah?"

"Cal?" Maggie's voice boomed from the speakers. "Cal, is that you?"

"Yeah," he said again, taking his hand gingerly from his forehead. "Yeah, it's me."

"You sound awful."

Cal looked in the rear view mirror. The skin of his face was the same wet-slate color as his hands, like he'd turned into an old-timey black-and-white photo, and his widow's peak seemed longer, bisecting his forehead and almost joining his eyebrows. His eyes were the color of maraschino cherries, vibrant against all that gray and black with just a black pinprick of pupils visible. He still looked human, he supposed, although it felt like he'd been caught in mid-transformation in a horror movie.

She had me draw to stop it, he thought. "Came down with something, I guess."

"Fuck," Maggie replied. "Right after your interview, too. Do you think you'll be too sick to work on Monday?"

Monday might've been next year for all Cal could comprehend at the moment. "I should be. I hope so, anyway."

"That's good," Maggie said. "Congratulations again, Calvin."

"What did you need, Maggie?"

"Oh." She sounded vaguely nonplussed, as if she'd been expecting to chat longer about Cal being sick just before starting a new job.

Look upon my works, Ye Mighty, and despair. What had that been from? Some dead poet he had to read in college. The line floated into his brain, and all of a sudden, he just wanted to sleep, shut everything down and go into the darkness for a little while.

She sighed heavily into the phone. "You're going to think I'm ridiculous."

Cal glanced at his bloodshot eyes in the rearview. "Try me."

"It's just...I was thinking about us going to Elise's grave, and feeling bad you weren't with us—"

Cal set his teeth at the word *us.*

"—and I took a nap and had the strangest dream."

He thought of Elise, in that impossible sunshine as he sat at his impossible desk, wearing his impossible suit. "Tell me about it."

"You were in your old condo," she began. "And you were sitting in that side chair I like, and Elise was sitting on the couch, but leaning over your coffee table, and she had this bunch of papers in her hand. And she was telling you how good the drawings were, and how you should focus on this over anything else because the drawings were *good* for you. She was real emphatic about it. And you were sitting there, in this really handsome suit, and saying that you couldn't. You couldn't draw because you were still too angry." She cleared her throat. "I woke up after that and thought, *I have to call Calvin.*" She sighed again. "I know, it's stupid."

Cal looked down at his strange hands in his lap. "It's not stupid, Maggie," he said, softly. "I dream about Elise all the time, too."

"Yeah," she said, and her sounded heavier than before. Wetter. She sniffed. "Are you still drawing, though? My god, I don't think I ever saw you anywhere without, like, a little pad you could slip into your back pocket." She chuckled, and it still sounded damp. "I think that was the most shocking thing about her school's memorial—not even the teacher's husband whaling on you, but you not having your sketchpad."

Let's just gloss over how that fight ended, he thought, hearing his own screams in his head. "I didn't have it at the funeral, either."

"No," and her voice was low again. "No, you didn't."

"I am still drawing," he said. "I didn't for a while, but I've started again. I needed something to focus on."

"That's *good*, Cal," she said with almost painful earnestness. "You're talented."

He looked around the parking lot, zeroing in on the Lexus next to the minivans. "Hey, listen, Mags, like I said, I *am* sick, and I kinda wanna go back to crashing out on the couch and watching television."

"Oh! Oh, sure, of course. Go rest up. I just...I just wanted to check in."

Cal lowered his head, closed his aching eyes. "Thank you."

"And you'll call me if anything goes wrong?"

I need to get off this phone and forget you're married to the man responsible for our daughter dying and forget that you treat me like I'm your other child and not your ex-god-damned-husband. "Of course, Maggie. Bye."

"By—" He hit the END button on the dash screen, then shivered. Goddammit.

He heard a sigh—

(you don't have to do this daddy)

—as he got out of the car. "You know I do, Elise," he said, and started across the lot. The itching started again, rolling up the backs of his arms, across his shoulders, down his spine. He could see what all this was doing to his face, his hands, but what was it doing *underneath*? It seemed his mind had split into two different spheres—one wholly focused on those responsible for his pain, and another, the part of art and new careers and just grieving for his daughter, that wondered about how this was changing him, and if it was permanent and the over-arching question of *why*.

"But whys don't matter when you're in pain," Cal muttered. "You just want the pain to *stop*. Whys come after."

The Lexus's interior was used-car-lot clean—neat, but obviously not new. Nothing that told him anything about the driver. He went to the cafeteria doors. The doorhandles lacked a trigger to depress. It had to be key-locked. He gripped it, anyway, thinking of how he'd thrown the drunk like loose laundry. The suit had done that.

(daddy)

YOU CAN'T SAVE WHAT ISN'T THERE

Her voice carried on the wind, but seemed to come from right next to his ear.

(daddy don't)

There—beyond the Honda's front bumper, in front of the season-denuded tree, a lightening and a warping in the shape of a small humanoid. Cal could still see the street and houses beyond it, but it was like seeing those things through a frosted, distorted glass.

(this is wrong daddy)

(you know what will happen)

(draw draw for me draw for yourself be healthy daddy)

Cal let go of the door handle. Again those two minds— the part almost exalted at seeing what he believed to be his daughter, somewhere from beyond—

(elise matheson and her incredible interdimensional journey, he thought*)*

—and the part that was...not *annoyed* to be interrupted, but distracted from his main goal.

"I can't stop until this is settled, Elise," he said. "I can't stop until I stop hurting."

(it won't—)

"We'll see," he cut her off. He closed his strange eyes, *squeezed* them closed, and when he opened them again, the apparition was gone. A sudden hole in his chest, as if a part of his heart had broken off and dissolved, brought scalding moisture to his eyes, but he turned back to the door, gripped the handle, and yanked.

The door was unlocked, the strength he used making him stumble. He peered into the dimness of the cafeteria, aided by glass doors at the opposite end that opened onto a courtyard. He let his eyes adjust, picking out the foldable circle tables, small enough for little people. Cal came out of the short hallway, the wooden stage a black hole to his immediate right. The two doors, more black holes, to his left for the lunch line, the doors to the far right that led to the gymnasium. He stepped into the center, picking out where he and the teacher's husband had fought, their blood smearing the tile. Whose blood had it been—his or the husband's?

Two hallways ran to the left and right of the courtyard doors, and Cal tried to reconstruct the mental map from when he came for parent orientation over a year ago. The building was a square, the hallways outlining the shape. The left led to the classes for the higher grades, eventually wrapping around the front for the kindergarten, first, and second graders. The right hallway led to what the school called "specials" classrooms—music, art, keyboarding—and eventually the main office.

Cal debated. The owner of the Lexus *could* be a teacher, coming in to do some necessary work that couldn't have been finished during the workweek...but it wasn't likely. Either that nervous fuck or the severe woman. He honestly didn't care who—both bore responsibility.

Cal weaved around the tiny tables, allowing the shadows of the hallway to consume him. The hall immediately took a hard left, opening up to autumn brightness at the very end where it spilled into the school's glass-encased main entrance. Classroom doors marched along either side.

YOU CAN'T SAVE WHAT ISN'T THERE

Just before the main entrance, the front office took the right corner, glass-fronted to give the office staff a view of who was beyond, dark save for an overhead light in a corner room beyond the main partition. The office door was open and Cal stepped inside. He heard the clack of an old computer keyboard and what sounded like soft classical music playing. He stopped at the doorway, just outside the room's light, watching the rotund man in profile, working intently on a desktop computer, the screen resting on a horizontal hard drive. He wore a faded polo shirt, the collar wilted. He squinted at the screen as he typed in a quick two-fingered manner. On the windowsill beside him, an old radio played the music.

"It's true what they say," Cal said, "that school employees really *are* more dedicated than other workers."

The man screamed, recoiling, and Cal looked at the nameplate on the door. Mungavin. Mr. Mungavin, Assistant Principal.

Mungavin cowered against the window sill, hands frozen in front of him in a vague warding-off gesture.

"*Who*—" he began, his voice piping. Cal stepped into the light and Mungavin's speech cut off with a brisk *snap*.

"But how dedicated were you when my daughter was killed?" Cal finished.

Mungavin's mouth worked, a gasping sound far back in his throat.

"You're going to help me," Cal told him, bringing himself to his full height, and, oh, the itching intensified, vicious little pricks against his changing skin, unpleasantly warm. "I want Flaherty's address."

Mungavin blinked at him.

"Now, you murdering fuck," Cal added.

Mungavin tried speaking. "I—I don't understand—"

Cal brought his fist down on the end of the desk, and, although he felt the mild pressure of impact, the desk tilted, the top cracking loudly and the legs buckling. The keyboard slid towards him an inch as the computer mouse jumped.

He repeated, "I want Flaherty's address. You remember Flaherty. She died with my daughter."

Mungavin's eyes widened until they seemed about to fall out of their sockets and roll down his soft cheeks. Cal leaned towards him. "You will give me the address. It was your procedures that allowed my child to die, put all those other children in danger, so you will give me the address. Nod if you understand."

Like a puppet wielded by an enthusiastic amateur, Mungavin's round head bobbed up and down.

"Good. Do it."

Hesitantly, Mungavin maneuvered his chair to face his computer again. He watched Cal with one eye as he clicked out of whatever he'd been working on, and double-clicked on another icon. He typed, moved the mouse to click around, typed again. Cal watched him sweat, dark stains forming along the sides of his polo shirt, wilting the collar further.

Finally, he moved the chair back to the windowsill, and resumed cowering. "Th-there. On the screen."

Cal stepped forward, leaning down. He saw the teacher's thumbnail picture—the same as what had been on the easel at the memorial—and took in the demographic information. He doubted the phone number was still viable. "Good."

"Whu-what happened to you?" Mungavin asked.

"Grief," Cal replied.

Mungavin's face took on a quizzical expression that reminded Cal of dumb, confused dogs. "What—"

Cal grabbed Mungavin's head and drove it into the computer's hard drive tower—once, twice, three times. The keyboard snapped in two beneath Mungavin's chin. The screen bounced and fell off the back, imploding against the carpet. Mungavin's collapsing forehead made a soccer ball-sized divot into the weak hard drive metal.

Cal shoved the corpse aside. The top of the skull knocked the little radio off the sill before starring the reinforced window glass. Cal stared at it. Mungavin's eyes were buried in deep bruises as dark as Cal's skin, goggling at nothing. His nose was pointed inward, blood coating his mouth, slack to show broken teeth.

"Good," Cal started to say, when the blanket of nails attacked him again. He cried out, hunching over and hugging himself. A battalion of serrated daggers sawed through him. He howled in the quiet confines of the school, shambling out of the office, finally collapsing onto his knees out in the hallway. He bore his teeth, seething, arms wrapped around his midsection like a straitjacket. He felt his pulse in his head, sledgehammer slams against the inside of his brow.

(daddy)

And then it stopped again, like his nerves, simply done with all of this, had flicked a switch. Cal fell limp and, through teary eyes, saw a dark shape down the long hallway.

(daddy you don't have to do this)
He shuddered, his body tingling.
(daddy you have to stop)
He squeezed his eyes closed, hugging himself again. The tile floor was so cool, so good, against his hot skin.
(daddy—)
"I can't," Cal croaked, his ruined voice wet and phlegmy. "I can't stop now."

He heard a sigh, and he opened his eyes. The hallway was empty.

Slowly, he sat up, got back to his knees, then, shakily, to his feet. He looked down at his hands—they were darker, the nails thicker and longer, pitch black in the gloom. A lunatic thought crawled across his head: *Don't think I could hold a pen now if I wanted to.*

From under his shirt cuffs, blood seeped down his arm, stringing around the narrow part of his wrist, lazily letting go of droplets onto the floor.

(whose blood whose blood)
He put a finger to it and hissed at the wire-thin jab of pain.

"Doesn't matter," he croaked. He started walking back up the hallway. He felt blood dribble into his palms. "None of it matters."

Sliding into the driver's seat, he glimpsed himself in the rearview. Baby spiral horns, thick bases that tapered a few inches away from his skull. Skin the color of coal smoke. Eyes now like smoothed rubies, jammed into irritated sockets. The seat felt smaller to him, as if he'd grown, widened, even as the suit felt as tailored as ever.

"None of it matters," he repeated, and started the car.

YOU CAN'T SAVE WHAT ISN'T THERE

The house sat in one of the city's outlying neighborhoods, a neat and tidy one-story post-war square. Someone with a green thumb had once landscaped the front yard, but that had been a while ago, and the mulch beds were overgrown with dying weeds, the shrubs unkempt, the dying lawn shaggy.

Cal parked on the opposite side of the street and unfolded himself from the car. He had the area to himself. It was as if the world had gotten cues and decided to keep out of his way.

(daddy)

He turned, and Elise sat in the backseat. She was far too pale—white paper made flesh, making the blue of her checked dress pop, her brunette curls almost black, in comparison—but she was *there*.

(daddy stop this)

And Cal turned away. He marched across the street, but, even as he did, a wave of weariness swept through him. This was his life, now. This suit, this changing body, this pervasive onslaught of grief and pain and anger. The idea that he'd been artist, a father—they felt like identities he'd tried on in a dream once and could only imperfectly remember.

He looked down at his monstrous hands. This felt realer, inescapable. And he didn't doubt his reasoning, his motivation, but a niggling feeling of *lacking* began to chew at the thoughts in the back of his mind, like there should be something *more* than this. But he had no idea what that could be, anymore. He had no idea what came after this. Grieving parents couldn't conceive of forever, any more than a child could.

He smelled burning leaves as he stepped up onto the curb, saw a fat tendril of grayish-white smoke trailing from the backyard. He moved up the driveway, around the Jeep Liberty parked in front of the chainlink gate separating the back from the front. In the yard, he saw Flaherty's husband, slumped in a plastic Adirondack chair before a wide, dug-in firepit that smoldered with dead leaves, the walls built with loose brick. A rake lay on the ground beside the pit. Flaherty stared at this, a beer bottle in hand. Four empty bottles lay like dead soldiers beside the chair.

Flaherty had subtly changed in the past seven months. The gray in his hair no longer looked so new. He wore the Carhartt coat, but it floated around him, like he'd lost weight. In his mind's eye, Cal saw Flaherty roaring above him, his face a rictus of grief and pain, raining down blows, screaming, *Where the fuck were you? It's your fault!*

Flaherty looked over as Cal approached, and his eyes narrowed. "Are you real?"

"I'm real," Cal replied, his voice like grinding stones.

"Can't tell, anymore. I see things. I see things sometimes. Not always real." Flaherty shook his head and finished his beer. He let the bottle drop to the ground.

"Your wife shouldn't have stood at the curb," Cal said.

Flaherty glared. "Fuck you. She was a good person. A good teacher. It was that fucking...that fucking drunk *driver.*" He raised his hands, seemed to study how they shook, then let them drop. "Should've executed *him.* Shoulda never let him near a car. Killed him in the crib. I don't give a fuck."

"He's dead."

YOU CAN'T SAVE WHAT ISN'T THERE

"Oh yeah? Good. Fucker."

"You blamed me," Cal said. "You said it was my fault."

Flaherty squinted at him, frowning. For a moment, all one could hear was the crackle of flames in the leaves, the soft sigh of the wind.

"You were late," Flaherty said finally. "What happened to you?"

"I wasn't supposed to be there. This is what happens when you decide to act on your anger."

Flaherty considered this. "Was it worth it?"

Cal heard a sigh, soft and mournful, not blowing with the wind, but in the center of his head. "I don't know."

Flaherty frowned. "Should've been there. Shouldn't be a widow at thirty-two. Shouldn't..." He trailed off, head lowering. Cal watched tears course down the other man's face.

That wave buffeted Cal's nerves again. This was forever. He thought of the two of them, each flying solo at the memorial, pummeling each other until their blood mingled on the tiled floor. Their reflective bellows of pain. The man before him was broken, had been broken so thoroughly, but was Cal any better? They'd both lost, hadn't they? Hadn't he been similar to this very thing only a few months ago, when some dim part of him realized he couldn't sit drunk forever, least of all because his savings couldn't allow it? Flashback, and he didn't have a firepit like Flaherty, but he had a television and a couch, and a part of Cal would've bet that they'd sat in similar postures. The man before him was a past reflection.

But the anger, that pilot flame in the furnace of his chest, warmed him. This *man* had *dared* blame him for the death of his daughter, this man whose spouse should've had the common sense not to stand so close to the road, not when she had the responsibility to protect her charges, and his daughter was dead because of *her*, and *this* man blamed *him*.

The weariness tried to hold him again, and he heard that sigh in the center of his head, but he fought against it.

Cal stepped forward, grabbing ahold of Flaherty by the armpits and lifting him out of the Adirondack chair easily. Flaherty's boots kicked the cheap plastic thing aside, and he squawked drunkenly. Cal held him high—

(the way he held elise high when she was a toddler)

—and snarled up at the crying, broken man. He slammed his new horns into Flaherty's neck, the spirals tearing through each side of the Adam's Apple. It hurt, they were still tender, and a punch of vertigo descended from the top of his skull. He felt hot blood rain onto his head, bathing him, and listened to the man gargle. He wrenched his horns out in a splash of gore and heaved the man over the firepit, sending him rolling and tumbling into one of the smaller leaf piles. Cal watched Flaherty seizure until finally, with a soft drumming of the heels of his work boots, Flaherty lay still.

"Done," Cal said. His hands flexed at his sides, black claws brushing against the rough leather of his palms. "Almost done." He still lacked any sense of guilt or regret, and that was good, but the satisfaction he'd felt when he'd seen Franklin's body didn't come, and Cal felt a hollow space in his chest where he thought it should be.

YOU CAN'T SAVE WHAT ISN'T THERE

It dawned on him that he hadn't felt it, either, when he'd dealt with Mungavin, but he'd been too distracted from the sudden surge of pain. Now, he just felt the hollowness, the weariness tugged at his mind.

Not as responsible, he thought, but it took effort to put the words together, like trying to muscle your way through a crowded room. *Franklin was responsible. Dennis is responsible. Flaherty, too, and Mungavin, but not as much as Franklin and Dennis.*

Was that it, then? The reason for the ennui that pulled at his nerves and muscles now? These last two bore fault, but not as directly as the others?

(because a part of you knows this is wrong daddy)

She spoke in the center of her head, but she stood back by the gate, the direction of the sun aping how he'd seen her in his dream. From this distance, she didn't appear as pale, as *unreal*, but he knew. He knew she wasn't there.

He stepped towards. "It was wrong what happened to you."

Elise cocked her head.

(i wanted you to have a chance daddy)

"A chance at what?" Approaching, the paper-white skin glowed in the autumn sunlight. "I'm nothing now. Nothing matters."

(you had a choice)

"I didn't choose this pain," Cal said, and walked through his daughter, who burst into a wisp of smoke that smelled of burning leaves. The tingling briefly surged across his skin, making him shudder. Reaching the curb, he felt momentum, an energy, seep back into his system like an IV drip. No, Flaherty's husband, Mungavin...they bore responsibility for what happened, of course, but not the brunt of the blame.

Franklin had. And he was dead.

Dennis did, and he soon would be.

"That motherfucker," Cal growled, marching across the road. He saw himself in the driver's side window, tall and monstrous, the horns now spiraling and curving back, and his red eyes blazed from his dark face.

He wedged himself into the car, the seat too small, his horns brushing the ceiling, so that he had to hunch forward to get room. It unzipped a pain, like a yellow stitch from running across his midsection, and acidic spit filled his monster mouth. He looked down and saw he was bleeding through his shirt, just above his belt.

What's it doing to you inside? the interior voice asked, now the voice of reason, the voice of the person he'd once been. *What's the suit doing to you inside?*

"Doesn't matter. It's almost over."

He waited, but Elise didn't sigh this time. He dropped the gear into Drive and pulled away.

The funeral itself was anti-climactic. Aside from an insistence that the ceremony be kept private, Cal had made no other demands, and Maggie and her extended family had organized the viewing, the gravesite service, the wake afterwards. They'd organized the timeframes and any speakers.

YOU CAN'T SAVE WHAT ISN'T THERE

No one asked Cal to speak. After the burst of almost hyper-real clarity at the memorial—scenes he might've painted then uploaded into Adobe to play with the contrasts in order to really bury the viewer in how surreal it was—he seemed to drift from each station on the Elise Matheson Is Dead Itinerary, his mind a hollow cave where the sighs of potential thoughts moaned but never arrived. He sat in a folding chair diagonal from Elise's coffin in the stuffy, blandly lit funeral home, unable to take his eyes off her. He rested his elbows on his knees, hands threaded together, as if in prayer.

No one tried to speak to him, and he didn't try to speak to anyone. He heard crying, and muttered conversations tinged with thick voices, but didn't know who'd done it. He had no family, had been estranged since he left home at eighteen, so the room was populated by Maggie's family and friends. Dennis's too, probably. He hadn't invited Jason, his old college roommate and the only person Cal could've considered a friend. He wanted to be alone with this. People distracted him from the pain.

The viewing ran for two nights, and Cal took the same position both times, from beginning to end, never moving. He hadn't started drinking, yet, that would begin in a month or so, and his thinking—as far as he was *able* to think—dealt with crafting his resignation letter from the ad firm, moving out of the condo to save money while he...but he couldn't quite finish the thought with *deal with this*, his shell-shocked mind skittering away from the concept, only teasing the edges.

The move, on the third morning, to the cemetery had been as muted, and he stared at the speakers—the funeral director, an at-home daycare owner Maggie had befriended, Maggie herself—without seeing them, his focus entirely on the gravestone with its *Elise Anna Matheson Loved Daughter April 11, 2014 – May 20, 2021* chiseled inscription, so new a part of Cal thought you'd cut your finger along the edges if you ran your hand over it. He *had* to look at the stone because the closed coffin, so small, so shiny, would've broken him fully and completely, the pieces never reassembling, and he couldn't allow that. Not here. Not in front of these people.

When the mourners drifted to the lane where the line of cars waited afterward, he wanted to be last, but Maggie lingered, as well. Dennis stood far away, beside her Audi.

"You're coming to the house, right?" she asked.

Cal hadn't gotten up from his seat yet, hadn't looked away from the tombstone. "Yeah."

He heard her sniff, swallow hard. "Oh, Cal."

"I'll be along," he told her. "Don't dawdle. I know Dennis's waiting."

He heard something click in her throat. After a beat, she said, "I know you. Please come to the house."

"I will."

"Dennis wanted to talk to you."

He didn't reply.

"Cal, he needs to talk to you."

"There's nothing to say, Maggie."

He heard her hiss. His eyes stayed on the stone. *Loved Daughter.* Of course Elise had been. Knowing but never really acknowledging it until now, she had been the absolute center of his existence, the reason he'd been made in the first place. Now what was he going to do? His center had been taken away.

Her voice almost unintelligibly thick, she said, "Please come, Cal...*I* need you there. She was *our* daughter."

And, finally, he looked away from the stone, at his hands in almost-prayer between his knees. "I know, Maggie. I'll be along."

A long moment, and then she just said in her watery voice, "Okay," and he heard her move away. He heard engines start and cars roll away, and he stayed put. He looked at the coffin now, at the shell, the empty center, locked within.

"Where are you now?" he whispered and oh god how he wished he believed there was some kind of eternal reward, some afterlife plane of existence, that his daughter could still be somewhere, that she wasn't completely and utterly gone like he knew she was. "What are you doing?"

He didn't cry. His eyes ached and felt gritty, like someone had rolled them in margarita salt and shoved them roughly back into his sockets, but he didn't cry. When he'd heard the news, of course, and he would spend months afterwards doing little else and then drinking until he passed out so it would stop, but not now. None of the people around deserved to see him like that. Elise hadn't been *their* reason for existence.

He drove to Maggie's home. Cars spilled out of the inclined driveway and along their side of the development's sleepy, curving lane. He parked along the opposite side, finding a space in front. He'd taken in the lit windows, in spite of it being only a little after noon, Maggie's Audi and Dennis's green Forrester parked in front of the garage.

His hand had hovered over the ignition, steeling himself for what was to come. He'd mentally roused himself by this point, coming back to the here and now, and he hesitated. He could see the hours stretching out before him—uncomfortable, politely fending off the overtures of mourners who would feel compelled to speak to him now that the rest of this sordid business was over.

He thought of Dennis, how his face would be stamped with its own kind of sadness—but not the amount of guilt Cal wanted the fucker to have, never the amount. Maggie said Dennis needed to talk to him, but Cal for the life of him couldn't think of a single thing he wanted that man to say. He'd been indifferent to Dennis up until this point, but now Dennis had firmly planted himself in Cal's life. He was the one who'd taken Cal's center. He was the one who'd sent Cal adrift.

But Dennis would get his opportunity, even if Maggie somehow had to mechanize the moment. Cal could almost imagine her locking them in a room together, she was stubborn that way, but Cal couldn't visualize it, the way he used to always visualize things, imagine them as art pieces—maybe a sketch, maybe a drawing, maybe a tinker in Photoshop.

Looking up at the house with its lights and too many cars, the spring sun just beginning its drift behind the roof, Cal...couldn't. He couldn't do it. Not the earnest overtures, not Dennis's fumbling and pathetic attempts to apologize, not Maggie's determination that This Had To Happen with intended initial capital letters.

YOU CAN'T SAVE WHAT ISN'T THERE

Cal pulled away from the curb, leaving the house behind. When a person loses a spouse, they're called a widow or widower. When a child loses their parents, they're called orphans. Cal was *vilomah*. He'd looked it up. It meant "against the natural order". It meant when a parent loses a child. And if anything was vilomah, it was watching his child getting lowered into the ground, it was knowing the man responsible wanted to painfully apologize for it, as if that could change anything.

And, now, Cal pulled his car into the same spot as he had long ago, with his back now aching from driving hunched over, a line of wet heat in his gut. He took in the house, lights not on and driveway empty except for Maggie's Audi and Dennis's Forrester. He saw the sun, now a late autumn sun, just beginning its drifting descent behind the roof.

With a clawed finger, Cal killed the engine and slowly unfolded himself from the interior, ducking his inhuman head to avoid his horns getting caught on the doorframe. He slammed the door and straightened, his strange spine crackling as it lengthened. He felt tender, sore...a mass of improperly used muscles and joints. But it did not matter. This had to happen.

Flaherty...Mungavin...they'd been indirectly responsible for what had happened to him, for making him vilomah. Franklin...Dennis...they were the *reasons*, the *cause* of this. They had pulled his center from him, turned him into this, and it made his fists clench hard enough to crack his knuckles, made his teeth grind, made his eyes harden.

He was finally here, and Dennis would know how vilomah felt.

(daddy STOP)

Cal jerked, as if he were a collared dog running to the end of his leash, and he flashed back to the moment when he'd first put on this damned suit, when he'd thought of how delighted Elise would've been, and his grief had come in a brief but terrible squall. Had it only been a day? It felt like an eternity.

He grunted, and saw Elise at the mouth of the driveway, fully present, not a glow or a distortion now.

(daddy stop this right now)

"It's too late, love," he growled. "This is what I am now, and I have to make those responsible pay."

She shook her head emphatically, the way she did when she was a toddler and didn't like something Mommy or Daddy told her.

(no daddy this is not who you are this is who you chose to be)

"I never chose *this*," he said, taking another step. "I couldn't take this suit off. This suit changed me."

Elise sighed, but her expression said she was about to start sobbing—her eyes wide, her mouth a thin stitch.

(daddy the suit was to save you)

"How?" he asked, still approaching.

Elise's lip quivered.

(to make you look handsome)

She inclined her chin, and what felt like a solid ball of wind slammed into his forehead, between the horns. Cal staggered, his vision swirling, and—

(he sees himself, but from a lower angle, a small child's angle, and he's fixing his tie in the mirror Mommy hung on

YOU CAN'T SAVE WHAT ISN'T THERE

the inside of their closet door. Daddy looks huge, a titan, but he keeps fussing over the tie, even as Mommy comes in from the bathroom, putting earrings on. "we have to hurry, Cal," she says. "don't want to be late to your own award, y'know?" "yeah, yeah," Daddy replies, shaking his head. "rah-rah-rah." "oh be proud of yourself—Elise is." and Daddy turns to see her, and his face breaks out in a smile. he lets go of the tie, buttons his jacket, and sweeps his fingers through his always-messy hair. "look good, love? ready for my picture moment?" and she giggles and nods, her view of Daddy pogo-ing up and down. "you look handsome, Daddy," and her Daddy is handsome, ready for anything, and she knows this is all because of his art, somehow, what he draws and does on the computer, and that makes her feel even better because she likes art, too, wants to do art like Daddy one day, and—)

—Cal screamed, not a bark or a howl or a snarl, but a human sound of pain. He dropped to his knees, hugging himself, in the center of the lane. He screamed again, a wet shriek. His chest felt like egg shell, cracking into smaller and smaller bits.

(i wanted to help daddy)

He lowered himself, prostrate, until his fevered forehead brushed the hot top. He squeezed his eyes closed and felt the tears spill, as hot as his flesh.

(i wanted you to feel better finally)

Cal slowly raised his head, and Elise was barely an outline, her silhouette a bluish-white, her center warping the driveway beyond, as if sending him that memory—and it'd just been his regular suit, the off-the-rack he'd always worn, the one he'd worn to her funeral, but Elise had never seen how loose it was, how basic, only how good he'd seemed in it—had taken something essential out of her, leaving just this light husk that could disperse with a moderate breeze.

Where are you now? he'd asked her grave. *What are you doing?* And, somehow and someway, she was here, had done this, and fresh heat filled his face.

"I'll never feel better," he whispered, and his voice was thick and gargled, but his own voice. Not the monster growl. He looked down at his hands and they were human, blood-smeared and dirty. He rolled them into fists and his nails had their everyday-look of being chewed on.

(you still have a choice daddy)

God, even her voice seemed barely there.

"Oh, love," he breathed. He sniffed. "There's no choice now. Not now. Not when you're gone. Not when—"

Maggie's voice, loud and shocked, *"Cal?"*

His head snapped up, and Maggie stood on the house's porch, hugging herself from the cold. "Cal, what the hell is going on?"

From behind her, Dennis appeared from the gloom of the house, his brow furrowed—

(like a Neanderthal beholding a smartphone, Cal thought*)*

—with confusion and concern.

(daddy—)

Just a whisper in his mind, and Cal got to his feet, glaring up the yard at them, at *him*, and it was like it'd been when he'd seen Franklin, how he physically moved forward as his mind's eye took him back, showing him the dumbfounded horror Dennis had expressed at the hospital, the dumbfounded guilt at the memorial and the funeral, the look of someone too stupid to understand how the thoughtless things they'd done could spiral so completely out of control.

But it was also *different* now than it had been with Franklin, because every movement brought pain like muscle cramps up and down his legs, his arms, his back. He felt hot blood course down his face, into his hands, and saw they'd become monstrous again, the humanity banished. His head took on weight as his horns regrew with the thick, organic sound of snapping carrots. Maggie screamed, but both of them froze like jacklit deer.

He stepped up onto the curb and Elise was completely gone. He snarled, *"Why were you LATE?"*

It *hurt* to go forward, but it was an *avoidable* hurt, wasn't it, none of this ever would've happened if Dennis had been responsible, if Dennis had understood the gravity of his duties, if *Dennis had been on fucking time.*

"You killed my daughter," Cal growled, and a part of him relished the pain, even as it increased, even as it felt every nerve was screaming and every inch of skin felt coated in blood, because no being could endure this type of pain for long, so he knew he was near the end, and all he could feel in response to that was relief. This wasn't eternity. This wasn't forever. This was just the end. "It's your fault."

Maggie snapped back to it more quickly, a brisk shake of her head, even if her expression still appeared to be that of someone struggling to comprehend. She came down the steps, approaching him, hands up and out. She'd always had a yard of guts. "Cal, I don't know what this is, but it's okay, let's talk about this, let's figure out what happened to you—"

His head snapped to her, and for a brief instant, he saw himself reflected in her wide eyes, how inhuman he'd become. He swiped her aside, sending her flying into the bushes. She cried out hollowly, the way someone does when the air's been knocked out of them.

Cal mounted the steps, and Dennis still couldn't move, his head inclining upwards to take in Cal's full breadth. Except for his head, he might've been a mannequin.

"You," Cal growled at him. He saw Dennis at the hospital, outside the ER, staring at the patch of carpet before the doors to triage. He and Maggie had gotten there before Cal, but Dennis had left Maggie with Elise in order to stare down at that same dumb carpet, and Cal, not knowing the details only that something horrific had occurred, had brushed right by him, hearing Maggie's sobs as he came through the doors. He'd read how characters lost all strength in their legs, but hearing Maggie's voice, how her cries easily overrode the chatter of others and the announcements from the intercom, he'd finally experienced it himself, and he had gone down, curling himself into the wall. That was when he'd known, when he'd felt the first rough touch of the crushing stone against his heart, and he'd screamed then for the first time.

All because of the monster staring at the ER waiting room carpet then, the monster that goggled up at Cal's new painful form now.

YOU CAN'T SAVE WHAT ISN'T THERE

"Your fault," Cal breathed, and he shoved Dennis against the edge of the door frame. Dennis flew back, cracking his head a good knock against the wood, and fell bonelessly inside the doorway, across the foyer. A bloody, too-large handprint smeared across the front of his Aeropostale tee-shirt.

"Calvin!" Maggie screamed from somewhere behind them, but it didn't matter now, none of it mattered. It hurt to move. He would kill Dennis like he'd killed the others, and then the pain would overwhelm him and kill him, too, and that was okay, that was what he'd wanted all along.

Dennis goggled up at Cal as he entered, probably not even knowing why this was happening, not understanding how his own actions had led to this, the choices he'd made. Cal dropped onto Dennis's stomach, knees to Dennis's sides, and Dennis jerked, the air whooshing out of him. Cal reached out and wrapped his hands around Dennis's throat, bloody fingers staining Dennis's skin pink.

"You did this," Cal said. "You did this to yourself. Your fault. My daughter would be alive if not for you."

Dennis's mouth worked, but Cal had no interest in hearing what the man had to say—not after the funeral, not at any time since. Cal panted, exhales misted with blood; his muscles felt like rocks, flexing only through the sheer force of Cal's will.

Dennis's tongue popped out of his mouth like the till of an old fashion cash register. Cal throttled Dennis, smacking the back of his head off the hardwood floor. Cal thought he could squeeze harder, pop Dennis's head like a tick—hadn't he thrown grown men like they were children? how much harder could it be to crush the fluttering skin and tendons holding this son of a bitch's head to his body?—but he resisted. He hissed blood onto Dennis's reddening face. Even as something inside Cal pleaded for this to be over, he needed Dennis to suffer. He needed Dennis to know a fraction of the pain that Cal had lived with every single day. Cal needed Dennis to taste what being vilomah was like.

Maggie's hands, grabbing and pulling at Cal's massive shoulders. His own pulse roared in his ears, making everything sound like it was coming from underwater. Dennis's face turned purple, his teeth biting down on his protruding tongue hard enough to draw blood, his eyes wide and bugging.

"Feel this," Cal said. His growling voice was muffled, was meaningless. "Feel this, you son of a bitch. Feel it."

"CALVIN!" Maggie screamed from miles away. "CALVIN, STOP THIS!"

I can't, he wanted to say, watching Dennis's eyes drift up and away from him, becoming less scared and more confused.

Fresh, searing pain surged through his shoulder, and his grip loosened, the world snapping back into focus. He arched his back, roaring, hands pawing at the new agony, claws brushing a wooden handle—

(???handle???)

—a fingertip sliding along a sharpened edge.

Before he could grab at the source of the pain, Maggie shoulder-checked him and sent him tumbling off Dennis's spasming body. He went sprawling, the angle popping the kitchen knife out and taking a chunk of monster flesh with it. He looked up and saw Maggie on her knees on Dennis's other side, getting his head up as he wretched and coughed blood. His neck was one large purpling bruise.

Still HERE, the thought came out as a bellow, and Maggie and Dennis both recoiled as Cal got to his knees, bleeding onto the hardwood. He hooked his massive hands into claws and oh god it hurt but it didn't matter. Nothing mattered. Nothing did any—

(DADDY)

His head whipped around, and she stood on the stairs just beyond Dennis's head, backlit by the window at the landing, her brunette curls afire. Just like in his dream.

(Daddy come with me)

"I can't," he said in a voice no longer within shouting distance of human. "I can't, love. Daddy can't."

"Calvin—" Dennis croaked, but Maggie gasped. Cal glanced at them, and saw Dennis staring quizzically at him, while Maggie looked up the stairs. She saw Elise, too. Elise was real, and, somehow, that hurt more than anything else.

"Elise...?" Maggie breathed, but Elise didn't look at her mother, only at Cal.

(you can Daddy come with me you have to try)

And, as if she brooked no argument, she turned and started up the stairs, and Cal swore he could *hear* the sounds of her Mary Janes on the risers.

Cal got to his feet, leaning in the archway with the living room. Every limb refused to cooperate willingly and a forest fire seethed in his back, but he gripped the stair banister and heaved himself up the steps, claws scratching the blood-smeared wood. His footfalls sounded like his heart-beat. Behind him, he heard Maggie say, "Oh my god, Calvin, what—what is—" But he didn't turn. This wasn't for her.

Elise disappeared around the corner, and Cal followed, turning to see Elise's closed bedroom door. A markerboard, set at what would've been Elise's eye level, was affixed to the front, with the message, *Elise Matheson has picture 2day,* in Elise's shaky handwriting. Neither Dennis nor Maggie had ever erased it.

Cal gripped the knob, smearing more blood, and let himself in. Elise stood in the center of a room frozen in time—the bed still made and Elise's stuffed animals, including Mr. Pudge, her bunny, holding pride of place in front of the pillow. The sunlight through the window beyond her little-girl's desk made Elise's edges sparkle, like she was limned in diamonds. She was *here,* as solid as she had been at the mouth of the driveway. She looked up at Cal with no fear and no surprise, only sadness.

"Elise," he growled, swaying on his feet.

She pointed to the mirror against her closet door.

(try Daddy it's not too late)

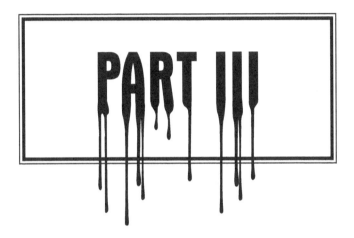

ou have to try, Daddy, *he hears her say.*

Cal holds his hands in front of him and tries to will them to change, like they had outside, as if to take back the choices he's made. He watches the monster in the mirror splays his fingers out, the black talons gleaming in the light from Elise's window. He tenses the muscles, stretches the tendons. But nothing happens—the pain doesn't abate, and his skin stays that wet-slate gray, bunched with muscle. It hadn't been him changing outside. It'd been Elise. He'd made his choices long ago.

He sees the thing he's become in the mirror, the suit still impeccably tailored to his hulking form, the white shirt an abattoir's smock inside his jacket, his monstrous hands coated in blood. His twisted horns nearly brush the ceiling. The pelt of hair, extending down from between his horns to the space between the red bulbous eyes of his expanded face, hangs limply. His cracked lips curl, disgusted, and, in the glass, he sees one wide fang appear. Every inch of him aches, the very extremity of his endurance.

She wanted me to try, *he thinks, and knows it is a child's wish, incapable of knowing how permanent things are. Both nothing is forever and everything is forever.*

A cool breeze touches his forearm, the pressure a comfort. It's okay, *she says. He can hear her with his ears now, not just in his head.* You tried, *she says, but he also hears what she isn't saying—that he'd tried too late, that his choice had led him here, that he owned this.*

He looks down, and she looks back up at him, wearing the same dress they buried her in, her brunette curls, dark fire. Her details are softer, now, her skin not copy-paper white, but a bluish-white.

I'm sorry, *he says in a voice no longer his own, like rocks grinding together. He hates the inhumanity of it.*

She keeps her hand on his forearm. It's okay, Daddy, *she repeats.*

But this isn't the resolution he wanted, he needed. He needed the pain to stop. He needed to be out of this damned suit. He needed all the things he'd done to be undone. He needed her to be alive again, he needed to not be vilomah.

Tears well along the bottom seams of his red eyes, hot and scalding, and he squeezes them closed. His knees buckle and he drops to the floor, twin thuds on the plush carpet that make the room shake. He feels the blood seep and patter off his fingertips, staining the floor, but that's all right. Let me bleed out, *he thinks.* Let me be done.

He hears the bedroom door open behind him—had he closed it? or Elise?—and hears Maggie gasp again, hears her say, "Oh my god, oh my god," *but it all sounds so far away. This hadn't been her story, her grief, and being in this room, Cal realizes the truth, how alike he'd been with Flaherty, how he should've seen it before, even at the memorial. He'd wanted to inflict his pain on the world, had been too wrapped up in himself to know the pain that the world itself had felt.*

But Elise had tried to help him. The suit had been a trap, yes, a concept only a child could think of, but it'd given him a choice. For the interview, for his art. If he'd drawn, he would've been okay—he'd seen that himself. If he'd just gotten through the Everest of his guilt, possible in this suit, he would've come out the other side. The suit wouldn't have been impossible to take off, would it, then? Impossible to know, now.

He opens his eyes and looks at his daughter, becoming fuzzier by the moment, and sees the truth. The suit became a shackle when he'd made his choice, the wrong choice, when he'd forced the world to feel his *pain and only* his *pain.*

"Oh Calvin, oh Elise," Maggie says, but Cal looks at his daughter and says the hard words he should've said long ago, I'm so sorry, love. I'm sorry. Daddy's sorry.

It wasn't your fault, she says, her eyes filled with terrible, awful understanding. You know that now, right?

He nods his misshapen head. He knows. He also knows what she isn't saying, couldn't say. Everything that happened after was his *fault. He bound himself to his pain and the suit delivered hellishly.*

More blood wells, from his shirt sleeves, through his shirt, his pantlegs. The beige carpet becomes sopping and lightness fills his head. This is the price you pay for what you do, *he thinks.*

She hugs him, and she's as solid as she's going to be, and he holds her tight, towering over her. She rests her head against his chest, a slight, cooling indentation against the hot, raw, wet flesh. Her forearms around his neck are two balms.

Let me stay like this, *he thinks, closing his eyes again.* Just let me stay like this, please oh god please, don't take her away again, not for what I've done.

But she fades, her form becoming more and more yielding until he's hugging himself, hunched over in the center of his daughter's bedroom, and he lays down on his side, his tears mixing with the blood on the soaking carpet. The lightness fills his head, and he hears Dennis, far, far away, "Oh Jesus, Calvin, hold still," *but it doesn't matter, not as his vision fails and the pain, finally and completely, subsides.*

He's alone again, and, alone, he goes into the darkness.

This is how the fairytale ends.

ACKNOWLEDGEMENTS

I'm going to be quick about this, but certain thank-yous need to be given. No work of art is done in solitude, not really. Directly or indirectly (usually indirectly), people encourage us, cajole us, hector us to put in the work, to get into gear, to do the absolute best with whatever talent we have, and that needs to be stated from the top. I'm writing this after doing a review of copy-edits and the emotions are running high, friends and neighbors. Bear with me; I'll try to be brief.

First off, massive thanks to Lisa Lebel, Dan Franklin, and everyone else at Cemetery Dance Publications. If you had gone back in time and told twenty-something Paul that, one day, he'd be working with one of the most venerated and storied genre presses around, he might've laughed in your face. There's a part of me that still can't believe this is something that's happened.

Thanks to Kevin Lucia for expressing interest and initially steering *You Can't Save What Isn't There* towards publication. None of this would've happened without him.

In addition to that, thanks to Brian Keene for indirectly putting me in touch with Kevin. While Kevin and I have known each other for a few years, it was through Brian's post-Bram Stoker Award party in 2023 that got Kevin and I talking.

Thanks to Chris Panatier, a stellar writer in his own right, for the *fantastic* cover and permission to use a line from your novel *The Redemption Of Morgan Bright*. My god, brother—you knocked the art out of the goddamned *park,* and I'm eternally grateful. To anyone reading this, go pick up the novel (and his earlier work *The Phlebotomist*). You're in for a hell of a treat.

Thanks to Patrick, James, and Laurel for the kind words about this very, very dark piece. They are all good writers in their own right, pardon the pun, and Laurel's novella *Crossroads* percolated through my mind during the writing of this story.

In no specific order, big thank-yous to the following people: Kieran E, Josh Z, Suzanne G, Brendan H, Todd K, Aaron D, Jessica M, Max B3, Michael B, and the Janz. None of these people know I'm thanking them here, Dear Reader Of This Vaunted Acknowledgements, and they might not even know why I'm thanking them. I'm telling you, though, it's because they gave me their friendship, their companionship, their space, and their time. Also, again, this is a Cemetery Dance book, and, goddammit, I'm going to make every word I say count.

Finally, a thank you that he probably doesn't expect (nor expected to have a book dedicated to him!) to writer Bracken MacLeod. Writing this novella, I kept thinking of his work *Come To Dust*, which also deals with the lengths a father will go to for their child (albeit for far different reasons and results). It's an amazing work from a monumental writer that I call a friend and a brother. Not only do I appreciate

YOU CAN'T SAVE WHAT ISN'T THERE

his words (enough that we wrote a damned novella together years ago—*How We Broke*, which I dedicated my half to the bug, my daughter), but also his counsel. When Chris showed me the cover art for this, I immediately sent it to Bracken to celebrate with, because Bracken understood. Bracken's someone I'm always glad to have in my corner.

And, before I go, a quick thank-you to *you*, O Dear Reader of mine, for coming along this trip with me. Take care of yourself. Hold space for a loved one, if you can.

—December 8, 2024
Northern Virginia